CAPTAIN SATAN:
A GHOST RIDES THE DAWN

# CAPTAIN SATAN
### KING OF DETECTIVES
TM

# A GHOST RIDES
# THE DAWN

*By William O'Sullivan*

ALTUS PRESS • 2019

## CHAPTER 1
## SOUVENIR FROM HELL

C ARY ADAIR set the highly colored volume on the table when the hall-buzzer of his penthouse apartment sounded in the stillness of the richly furnished room.

From behind the costly Chinese screen at the far end of the long room appeared a gaunt, sad-eyed man dressed in severe black. Adair's keen eyes shot him a quizzical stare.

"Don't answer for a moment, Jeremy."

"No, Mr. Adair."

Cary Adair, whose main object in life was apparently that of occupying his hours in the pursuit of nothing in particular, shrugged the broad shoulders that were cloaked beneath a faultlessly cut morning coat. He passed a strong hand over his carefully combed hair and considered.

"I don't know that we should admit anyone so rude as to call at this hour." He snapped back a starched cuff and consulted his watch. "It's not yet noon," he said.

Jeremy's long, morose face was sympathetic. "A pity, sir," he murmured. He coughed slightly. "Not that we have many visitors at *any* hour, sir. There's your friend, Mr. Desher, sir—of the W.P.A."

"The F.B.I., you mean," Adair corrected him.

Jeremy sighed and stroked his chin with remarkably long, sensitive-looking fingers. "Of course, sir—the F.B.I. There are

A voice called, "It's the F.B.I.,

Satan—stay where you are!"

so many *initial* organizations now, sir—'A.A.A.'; 'F.H.A.'; and there's your friend, Mr. Desher, sir—of the Federal Bureau of Investigation—"

The buzzer sounded again, louder this time.

Adair's strong mouth curved in a smile. "As you say, Jeremy—

*there* is my friend Mr. Desher. Nobody but a government employee could be so impatient as to ring that way." He turned and paced down the thickly piled, priceless rug toward the great studio window that overlooked New York Bay.

"Take it, Jeremy."

"Yes, sir." The manservant crossed to the hall beyond the portièrs and lifted up the telephone. "You may come up, Mr. Desher," he said into it, before the other voice had a chance to speak. He hung up again.

Adair and his valet-butler stood watching a small lamp that glowed softly in a corner of the room, its gentle, rosy light falling on a shelf of rare old books. No sound came through the quiet-cushioned walls of the place.

But suddenly the color of that lamp light had changed. It had changed from a pink to a red. Adair nodded his satisfaction. "It works splendidly," he murmured. "Open the door for Mr. Desher, Jeremy." And simultaneously there came a loud rapping from beyond the portières.

Jeremy glided silently out of the room. A hearty voice broke the cultured quiet of the place, a voice that had a world of vigor, of power, of energy.

"…Jeremy! By Gad, man, it's good to see you! How's that loafer-boss of yours?"

"Mr. Adair is in the living room, sir," Jeremy answered frostily. "Your hat and topcoat, sir."

But Adair hadn't moved. He stood watching the lamp closely. The light changed back to rose-pink again as the portières of the foyer hall were swished back and Desher walked in with heavy tread.

"Well, Cary!"

"Jo!" Adair crossed the floor smoothly, his deceptive bulk riding lightly on those muscular columns of legs encased in the striped trousers. They shook hands. "Glad to see you, man." He yawned slightly. "It's genuine excitement to talk with an active man like you, Jo."

The Department of Justice operative stared around at the luxury of the place and grinned maliciously. "I can believe it." But he sobered suddenly. "How the devil did Jeremy know I was ringing that buzzer from the hall sixty-five floors below?" he asked.

Adair shrugged. "I don't have many early morning callers.... You're the only man rude enough to ring that early—and it's high time you were calling on me again, anyway."

Jeremy had been overlong in the foyer. Now, he crossed the room rapidly but silently, a flat packet in his hand. Adair's eyes left Desher's face to look at his servant, over the F.B.I. man's shoulder.

"Develop them," he said quietly to Jeremy. He turned again to Desher.

Desher frowned. "What's that? Develop what?"

Adair smiled slightly when Jeremy reappeared instantly with two cups of steaming Java and a decanter of brandy. "Develop us two *café royales*, of course. Makes a splendid eye-opener."

"My eyes have been open since four o'clock this morning,"

Desher growled sourly. "I'm a working man. I'm not a filthy-rich, coupon-clipping man-about-town like you!"

"Tough luck," Adair grinned. He pressed a wall button and the wide studio window folded back silently into its frame. "Come out on the terrace and tell me what is so important that the eyes of the F.B.I. must keep such ungodly hours."

DESHER WALKED to the guard wall of the colorful, tiled terrace. He sniffed eagerly at the clean, bracing air, squinted his eyes up at the sunny, June-blue sky.

Far below them ant-like crowds dotted the floor of New York's financial canyon. Automobiles dwarfed to the size of hardshell bugs scurried along tape-wide streets. Far up the Hudson river, the George Washington bridge seemed to strain its skeleton frame in a successful effort to hold the two shores immovable. The bay was like a pampered child's bathtub, with its miniature tugs and barges and steamers and ferries.

Desher shook his head enviously. "I have to give you credit, Cary. Once, I thought you were crazy, to buy a skyscraper just so you could take over the roof of it and live up top here." He turned. "Must set you back a pile of money to run it, eh?"

Adair fingered his wing collar. "On the contrary, the tenants pay *me*. I haven't a vacant space in the building—but I do have absolute quiet at night, the best possible view of New York Bay and no fussy, prying neighbors." He gestured widely with one arm.

"And where else could you be so near Newark Airport—so close to a bridge to Long Island—so close to *everything?* Grand Central station and the Pennsylvania lines are only a matter of minutes from me." He pointed. "Ocean steamers there—coast-wise steamers there—"

Desher chuckled. "All that, so you can forget about it, eh? Hell, man, you don't get around as much as a snail with rheumatism!"

"I go hunting every now and then," Adair protested. "How about that?"

"Yeah! How about it?" Desher scoffed. "You go hunting while I stay up nights and days tracking down criminals, murderers, bank-cracksmen, munitions smugglers—*and madmen!*"

Adair frowned. "Madmen? *Madmen,* you say, Jo?"

Desher nodded somberly. He leaned his stocky frame against the terrace wall, stared down into the streets with puzzlement in his brown eyes.

"You know, Cary—every now and then we come across a crazy pattern, in our work. Usually, it's cracking down on men who blow a national bank, or jumping kidnapers, interstate hijackers and the like. The setup in those cases is a pattern, understand? There's a certain sure bit of felony, to start with. You try to get fingerprints, the car licenses of the bandits, a description of them, their footprints, knee prints.

"Then, with those things, you start your tracking, checking the records in our Washington bureau. Or, lacking them, we send undercover men to criminal haunts, set dictaphones to catch the conversation of suspicious characters, set our men up in certain mobs, even." The man paused, his face suddenly weary, his eyes framed with circles of sleeplessness. "But in an affair like 'The Emperor of the Dead,' now—that's different!"

" 'The Emperor of the Dead?' " Adair repeated, his eyes wide. "Is that the story you've come up to tell me, Jo?"

The F.B.I. man shook his head. "That's the story I've come up to hear *myself* tell you. What in hell good does it do me to tell *you* things? You listen, yawn and go off on another hunting expedition!"

"But I listen," Adair smiled slightly. "I play a perfect Watson to your Sherlock Holmes. You're the worker—I'm the interested bystander. You're Bergen and I'm Charlie McCarthy."

"Now you're talking," Desher laughed. "You have a wooden head like Charlie, but you don't sit on my lap."

Adair laughed and led the way inside again. Jeremy had just passed the table where Adair had set down his book. Now, there were two framed photos on it.

Desher glanced casually, then stiffened. "Say!" He walked over and picked up one of the photos—one that showed a chunky, powerful man with a low, snap-brim hat and a light topcoat. It was in silhouette, in cutout shape, against a white ground.

It was Jo Desher, of the F.B.I.

The man blinked, turned to stare at Adair. But his host didn't see; he was lighting a cigarette. The Federal agent said, "Cary! Where and when did you get this picture?"

Adair blew out a cloud of smoke. "That? Oh, I dunno. You must have given it to me at one time. Eh?"

Desher's face was taut. "When did I last see you?"

His manner was gruff, uncordial. Adair veiled his eyes. "Several months, I judge."

8

"Right! And I got this coat only two days ago! What's the mystery, Cary? How did you come by this?"

Adair dropped into a chair. Jeremy materialized from behind the screen and set a solid gold coffee service on the small table. He picked up the frame, twisted around as if to get a better light on the photo. He brushed his lapel lightly, set the frame down again. He spoke; but to Adair.

"I beg pardon, sir? I believe Mr. Desher is mistaken, sir—about the photo. He is wearing a topcoat of light color, today, sir; and the one in our photo is *dark!*"

Desher glowered. "What? What the devil do you mean, it's dark?" He snatched up the frame again, squinted—and started suddenly. "By the Lord, so it is!" He rubbed his eyes with a stubby fingered hand, looked again. "What the hell!"

His gaze fell to Jeremy's hands; then he looked behind the table, under the chair. Adair smiled covertly.

"Oh, sit down, Jo, and relax. You're just overtired."

DESHER GRUNTED. He poured himself a stiff jolt of brandy and downed it. "Get yourself ready," he warned, settling comfortably in his chair and jamming a wickedly black stogie between his lips.

He let Jeremy strike him a light, then he put the cigar down on a tray to fish some papers from his inside pocket. He stuffed the other papers back in his pocket and reached for his cigar.

Desher hunched forward on the edge of his chair. "Get this, Cary," he said. "Three extortion letters have been written to men in three separate parts of the country—*'Pay or you die!'*—

the usual sort of note. All three men are very wealthy and inform us of the notes. One man pays his extortion, but denies it!"

"How do you know?" Adair asked. "How can you figure that if he doesn't admit it?"

"That's easy. We checked all three bank accounts. One of them drew heavily on his. The other two didn't." Desher paused.

"And?"

"We guarded the homes in every conceivable way. But the two men who balked were burned to crisps in their houses, at night. *And there's not a single clue as to how, or who did it!*"

"But—your men?"

Desher's face was grim and forbidding. "Four of *them* were burned to death! I'll get the mob behind this if it's my last living act!"

Adair blinked. "But—nothing unusual otherwise? Just—routine?"

"Remember what I said about crazy patterns? Here it is—in each case a flaming comet was seen streaking across the sky right after the fire started. In each case, a note of black paper of some sort was found in the ashes of the house—a 'signed' note—signed by the blackmailer. And that signature is identical with one found near a murdered United States Navy spy." Desher opened a black paper, held it out. Adair took it gingerly by a corner.

In brilliant red across the page was sprawled a lizard design—a lizard with mottled spots. And under it, scrawled in blood-red color, was the signature:

*The Emperor of the Dead.*

Adair stared at the thing, turned it over, sniffed at it ginger-ly. "What a peculiar odor," he exclaimed. "As if it were burned! And yet—"

"The Bureau is checking it to find what it's made of," he said.

"Oh. This is an extra one?"

"Right. I have it up here to check on the coloring matter used in making the drawing of that lizard. It must be great stuff to live through flame! Ought to be easy to check, from that angle."

Adair studied the affair again, got to his feet and crossed over to his books. He scanned the titles, selected one and opened it. After a moment, he snapped it shut. "That's what I thought," he said, turning to Desher.

"What?"

"This isn't a lizard."

Desher's brows went up. "That isn't a lizard? You're crazy!"

"Jo? D'you ever hear of a thing *like* a lizard—one of the lizard family, in fact—that has a moist skin, and was supposed by the ancients to be able to live in fire?"

Desher thought. He looked up suddenly. "A samovar!" he said.

Adair smiled. "A *samovar* is a metal urn used in Russia for making tea." He tapped the paper he held. "But you're close, Jo—this lizard-like thing is a salamander. A salamander is said to be able to live in the flames of Hell itself." He paused, con-sidered. "A fiery comet, seen by night over a flaming estate—a bit of paper that lives through flames—and the 'Emperor of the Dead.'" He shrugged. "There's your connection, Jo—do you see? What else could live in Hell's fire but a salamander?"

A peculiar tightness and excitement passed over Desher. He jumped up.

"*Satan!*" he barked.

## CHAPTER 2
## THE HALL OF DEATH

FLARES FLICKERED along the rough-hewn walls of the great, dark chamber. The smoke hung heavily in the frosty air of the place.

In the center of the bare, dirt floor glowed a fire of red hot coals. The fire was oblong in shape, about the size of an ordinary floor mat. Beside it crouched a deformed hunchback of a man, crooning a tuneless chant and fanning the coals with his bare hands.

Despite the cold of the place, other than where the fire builder crouched, four other men stood similarly clad—in brief breech-clouts. Their brown skins glistened in the light of the flares as they swayed from side to side in time with the hunchback's chant.

Directly facing these five was a rough-made throne, raised on a dais, and on this sat a slender, ascetic-faced man. His skin shone yellowish-white in the half-light of the dungeon. A white turban was wrapped around his head and an end of it hung down over one shoulder. His thin mouth was wide, and the lips slightly parted. The flares cast a dancing light over his face, raising and lowering the shadows of it and making his mouth seem in perpetual motion.

But no sound escaped those thin lips until the chant of the fire builder had grown loud, until the figures along the wall opposite swayed more noticeably. Then, in a sing-song oriental tongue:

"Bikko!"

None answered; but the fire builder came to his bare feet slowly. Still chanting, he swayed slowly to one end of the glowing oblong and calmly walked through the furnace heat of the coals.

"Ivan!"

One of the four brown men moved, then followed Bikko through the fire. He was husky, slant-eyed, low-browed, with a cruel scar that ran from his mouth down across his chin.

"Kanyo!"

A stout little man, his eyes glistening black as his long-cut hair, followed. A grimace of pain started on his lips; but yellowed teeth drove into the thick lip to still it.

"Corsi!"

A slender-limbed but paunchy man followed through the fire. Some burning coals had been scattered beyond the edge of the oblong by the feet which had trod over them. The man called 'Corsi' stopped mid-way across, calmly leaned over to pick up the glowing coals in his hands, and dropped them back into the heart of the fire.

"Datsu!"

A tall, clean-cut brown man swayed slightly more; but held

against the wall. His eyes slid right and left, flashing in the light. His mouth was parted, his breath came fast.

*"Datsu!"*

The figure along the wall trembled, buckled pitifully at the knees, made a brave effort to steady. The three who had preceded him through the burning coals ranged back along the wall opposite the dais-throne, their eyes lowered.

A sigh started gustily from the lips of the enthroned man, a sigh that started gustily and lingered for seconds on the still, cold air of the dungeon. The man with the yellow-white skin and ascetic face swayed to his feet, a deep chant issuing from his lips.

Slowly, with a majestic tread, he approached the blazing mass of coals, slowly mounted it with his bare feet, walked steadily, unhurriedly through the glowing mass. He paused a moment before he stepped to the cold earth again.

"Fire cleanses," he said slowly, in English. Then, in an oriental tongue, "Fire cleanses! The wicked fear the flames, shall perish in them."

"It is so, sire," four men responded, in both tongues. "It is so, sire. Fire cleanses. The wicked fear the flames, shall perish in them."

But Datsu cowered back against the wall, his face a mask of fear, his voice choking. "Sire—I—I—" he stopped, swallowed a sob. "I was burned by the comet. Truly, sire."

"Seize him—to be cleansed!" the hollow-voiced one spoke.

"No! *No!*" the man called Datsu screamed. "Sire, I beg you, let me—" His voice was throttled off as Bikko, the fire builder, threw a muscular brown arm around his shoulder, drew it tight in a choking vise. The other three assisted.

With the one addressed as 'Sire' leading, the others followed, the strangling man fighting desperately for his life. A roaring sound came clear as they neared the end of the dungeon. A panel of glowing metal with a red-hot handle stood out clearly in the wall. It was behind this that the roaring grew and died, grew again. The smell of hot metal was stifling.

*"Cleanse him!"*

Bikko grabbed the glowing handle in his bare hand, wrenched the metal panel back on its hinges. A roaring mass of flames leapt out into the room. There was a twist… a grunt… a flying brown body that was enveloped in flames… and a long-drawn, horrible scream. The metal door banged shut.

"He is cleansed," the hollow voice said.

A BELL sounded dimly in the cavern. Bikko bowed to the enthroned man and went quickly to a niche in the wall.

"Who speaks?" he asked in a low, vibrant voice.

He listened a moment, turned to the man on the throne. "It is Marku, sire. He calls from New York. He has followed the American detective and reports him at a friend's home. The man-of-the-iron-boats from across the sea is also following. The American detective is to die shortly."

The leader considered. "Tell him to learn what he can, then report to me here. Tell him, also, that his emperor commends him for his zeal. The two impure ones who worshipped their gold have been cleansed."

"Yes, sire." Bikko spoke in oriental tongue. "It is done."

"Bring me my maps, Bikko."

"Yes, sire."

The husky brown man spread on the floor three large maps which he took from under the raised dais. A wand appeared in the whitish man's hand as if by magic. The tip of the rod touched at four spots.

"…Here… here… here… and here! Four impure ones who must be cleansed, Bikko."

"Yes, sire."

"It is not for the possession of the gold that we—ah—cleanse them, Bikko. It is that their greed for the gold, their unwillingness to lose it, marks them as impure. They shall be cleansed."

"Yes, sire."

"And all who interfere with my cleansing shall know the purifying touch of the flame. They shall be cleansed in my name—in the name of The Emperor of the Dead and in his sign—the salamander!"

"It has been spoken," the four henchmen of the Emperor said solemnly. "Those who interfere with The Emperor of the Dead shall be cleansed!"

IN NEW York, an inoffensive little man with a pleasant smile and anxious, glistening black eyes, stood before the closed door of a private elevator in a large downtown skyscraper. He signaled the nearest hall attendant.

"I verre sorry," he said brightly, his teeth showing in a wide smile. "Pliss to open door to lift?"

The husky attendant looked. "Huh? Lift? Oh, you mean the elevator. That's private, buddy. You know the man who owns it?"

Black-Eyes continued smiling. "Pliss, I wish to surprise. Pliss to open." He made a movement inside the neat cape that was slung over his shoulders. The hall attendant looked down casually, his gaze attracted by the movement. And his eyes started out of their sockets.

An ugly looking automatic was snouting out at him.

"Pliss, I mean no hurt. I just verre anxious for speed. You open door, no?"

"Y-yes," the attendant stammered. "S-sure, Mike. I mean, Togo." He took a key from his pocket under the brown man's carefully watching eyes and slid the locked elevator door open.

"Pliss to come, also," the little, man said, his smile friendly as ever. The attendant stepped in the car briskly; but before the door could shut, another voice spoke—spoke in good English.

17

"Do not look around, please, Kokamori! I think I shall ride, too. When the door closes, I shall permit you to drop your gun to the floor—*if* you are very careful!"

The little brown man's grin turned to a sickly one; but he stood rigidly still. The newcomer was a squat, powerfully chested yellow man. His slate eyes were nasty. In his wide, gloved hand he held a businesslike .45 caliber automatic. His flat, wide face was expressionless when the small brown man's gun thudded to the floor of the elevator.

He motioned to the uniformed attendant. "Pick up gun, pass to me, press button to run lift," he said in a monotone, and the operator obeyed.

The operator stared with dazed, stupid eyes at each man in turn, then said dully, "Mr. Adair don't like nobody to come up without bein' announced."

The little man saw the humor of the attendant's foolish remark. But his smile was sad. The yellow man blinked. "Adair? Who is Adair?"

"Aw, just a guy that loafs around. He lives up there."

The yellow man grinned evilly. "In a few moments," he said softly, "it will be more correctly said, 'When Mr. Adair was alive, that was his home!'"

The attendant shuddered. The small brown man who had been greeted as 'Kokamori' seemed to shrink further into his loose cape. The elevator sped swiftly and noiselessly up the sixty-five stories. It came to a stop gently. The door swung silently and automatically open.

The yellow man stepped back carefully, his gun at ready.

Kokamori followed, stepping as if on eggs. The attendant sidled past the gun warily.

"No noise, please," the yellow man said flatly. "I do not wish to kill any more men than are now in that apartment." He pulled a cream-colored, transparent cylinder from his pocket and stepped to the door.

"Quiet!" he said softly. "I listen a moment!"

## CHAPTER 3
## THE SIGN OF DEATH

ADAIR SWUNG to stare at Desher, then laughed. "What about Satan, Jo? I thought you had seen him, the way you yelled that out!"

The F.B.I. man shook his head. "No, by God! But I'd like to. Cary—you've given me an idea. Remember, you said 'What else but a salamander can live in Hell's fire?' The answer is—Satan. *Captain* Satan!"

Adair shook his head despairingly. "Good old Jo and his Captain Satan!" He held up a hand when Desher started to interrupt angrily. "Oh, I believe you, Jo—I'll accept Satan as one of your playmates. But, you must admit this stuff is fantastic."

"So is Satan fantastic, Cary." Desher picked up his stogie-cigar and puffed hard to get it going again. "Gad, I tell you the man is incredible. Speaks about every language you ever heard, can crack a safe or dance a rhumba—can fight like hell—do practically anything!"

19

The screaming victim was forced before the open door.

Adair took it up, laughingly. He paused suddenly. "I think you saw him out West not long ago, didn't you, Jo? How old does he appear, Jo? Thirty? Forty-five?"

Desher sat suddenly still, his eyes steady. "Who told you I'd seen him?" His voice was low, careful. There was an element of hidden excirement in it. Adair dropped his eyes, appeared to consider.

"Didn't you tell me?"

Desher shook his head. "I shouldn't have, if I did." He became enthusiastic again. "But Satan's in this some place, Cary. I'm telling you!"

"Funny how many things you forget, Jo—about Satan. As I recall it, he uses a Satanic brand or something to advertise his wares, and not a salamander."

Desher was crestfallen. "Yeah, he does. But all the same—"

Adair went on: "Besides, you tell me he doesn't go in for any crooked work, that he's a gang smasher, a racket buster, a sort of one-man police force who tries to beat you lads to the punch and then pockets the crooks' swag. That right?"

"I shouldn't tell you so much," Desher growled. "You spoil all my pet theories."

Adair shrugged. "You have no theory this time, have you? You say yourself it's a crazy pattern. But, I can't imagine the man you describe to me as Satan burning people up in their homes. And for extortion, at that. It sounds phony to me."

"Oh, yeah?"

"Oh, yeah! And how about the United States naval spy who was killed—with the salamander mark, the mark of The Emperor of the Dead near him. You think Satan's gone in for that, too?

Desher surrendered. "No."

21

CARY ADAIR ground his cigarette out in the ash tray. "Any idea why that navy spy was killed?"

Desher nodded. "He was nosing into a strange helium situation. We've had undercover news that the Japanese are getting helium shipments from the United States."

Adair sat forward. "Helium gas? The gas that won't burn, that's wanted for use in dirigibles, in Zeppelins?"

"Yes," Desher said. "The government clamped a lid on it. We have virtually a monopoly on it—at any sort of reasonable cost of production, that is. We let down the bars, recently—but only for very limited use. This Japanese rumor has us wondering."

"Hm," Adair mused. "I suppose you've been checking the main sources? Amarillo, Texas? Thatcher, Colorado? Dexter, Kansas? They're the only fields where natural gas wells contain sufficient helium to be practicable, aren't they?"

"Say!" Desher blinked. "Where do you get all this dope?"

Adair chuckled. "What else do I do, but read? Hydrogen has greater lifting power; but it burns. Helium is one-tenth the weight of air, hydrogen one-twentieth. No gas well discovered yet contains more than two percent helium gas, in the raw. Helium is—"

"Let up, let up," Desher groaned.

"Okay," Adair grinned. "Now:—is there any way the helium gas could be stolen or drained off at those places? Or shipped from other places where it has been sent legally? Any chance of that?"

"I don't know and I don't care," Desher snapped irritably.

"What has that got to do with me? That's Navy Department business."

Adair smiled covertly. "You're not interested in that angle, eh, Joe? Not a bit?"

Desher shot him a keen glance; but he didn't speak.

"What about the comet business?" Adair asked. "Do you attach any significance to the fact that the comets were seen on the nights of the fire?"

Desher considered for a long moment. "Now, Cary—" his manner was apologetic, pleading almost. "*I* don't place any belief in it, mind you—but more than one man has said that there's something *weird*, supernatural, almost, in the fact that comets have appeared directly over the homes destroyed and that those strange '*Emperor of the Dead*' notes have been found when every other thing in the place was burned to a cinder!"

Adair was lost in thought for some moments. Then: "Well— it's interesting, anyway, Jo. Very fascinating, I must say." He yawned elaborately. Desher sensed it was time he must be leaving. He got to his feet, picked up the book from the table. And wrinkled his face.

"What's this, Cary? A book in Yiddish?"

Adair chuckled. "It's the *Arabian Nights*… in Iranic—or Persian. I find I get a fuller flavor of any book, if I read it in its original language. Russian… Japanese… Chinese… all languages have words that have *colors* that cannot be transmitted satisfactorily in any other tongue."

Desher grunted. "Wasting time studying Chink and Jap talk, eh?"

"Call it that," Adair said. "It amuses me, entertains me, and—" He stopped abruptly, his eyes narrowed to slits.

The little lamp in the corner had changed suddenly from a rose glow to a bright red. Somewhere near, a gong sounded faintly.

…And Jeremy had materialized in the center of the room, his eyes riveted on those closed portières, a hand at either hip. DESHER STARED from one to the other of the two. He became aware for the first time of the peculiar, red glow in back of him. "Say, what's going on here?" he asked.

*"Shut up, Jo!"*

Desher started at the tone—low, intense, commanding. He saw Adair's neck swell, saw a vein throbbing in the man's throat. But he was dumbfounded when he saw Jeremy's hands flick, saw twin automatics bloom suddenly in the man's hands.

"Someone outside?" Desher asked, his eyes narrowing.

Adair nodded. "Burglars, probably, Jo. Hijackers. We keep quite a bit of change up here."

"But, did you hear something?" The Federal man turned, looked keenly at the light. "Ha! An alarm hookup, eh?" But he wasn't answered.

Adair snapped a switch and the studio window folded shut. He pulled a cord and heavy, black drapes slid across the window frames, blotting out all light in the room—save for that tiny, red glow in one corner. The two men, master and servant, moved in the half-light like wraiths.

Adair spoke low. "The gong rang, Jeremy! That means more than one man is out there—listening to hear what's being said here!" He swung to his friend. "Talk, Jo! Talk about helium, about those fires, about anything. Make out you are *two* men carrying on a conversation!"

"Say! Who the hell are you giving orders to? I'm a government—"

*"Talk!"* Adair snapped. "Talk now, and we'll argue about it later."

Desher shrugged. "I think you two are crazy. It's simple enough to 'phone downstairs, trap whoever is out there!" But he humored Adair. "—You understand about those fires, eh, Cary?"... Then, deeper, "No; not entirely, Jo. I'm interested in that helium angle you mentioned—"

At a nod from Adair, Jeremy went forward stealthily, drew the portières quietly, without so much as a whisper of the material. Adair backed into the shadows of the far wall, his right hand sliding under his coat lapel.

"...What *of* the comets?"... Desher was talking for himself again. But his eyes bulged when he saw Adair slide an automatic from a shoulder holster... saw Jeremy tread back, catlike, and drop to a kneeling position on the floor in front of his master.

Desher, still talking loudly, braved his host's wrath to walk over where he could get a view of that darkened foyer... and the entrance door beyond it. He was aware that Adair's hand had felt along the wall, pressed at a button.

But he blared an oath when the foyer door snapped back and brought the smashing picture to his eyes. He went for his gun.

There was a frightened building attendant in uniform, his hands high over his head; a small, brown man in a cape, a sickly grin on his face; and standing close to the door the squat, powerfully-built, flat-faced yellow man—gun in one hand, a peculiar cream-colored cylinder in the other.

But Desher's amazement and surprise were no more than that of the stocky, yellow man in the hall, when the door swung open. Standing in the bright light of the small hall, he was squinting his eyes into the interior, was handling his gun as if searching for a target to shoot at.

A deafening crash echoed through the room. A spurt of orange flame stabbed through the darkness. The yellow man cursed in classical Oriental blasphemy, his shattered hand trying to get the gun up again.

Adair saw the convulsive jerk of the wounded man's hand, saw him yank the trigger despite his wounds, heard the scream of the slug and the *spat* with which it flattened on the wall behind him. He aimed carefully, pulled the trigger again.

The gun spun out of the man's hand, and he staggered. Jeremy cursed softly and methodically and fired with both hands. The yellow man's hat zipped off his head; and the cylinder in his hand seemed to burst.

There was a flash, a dull explosion that blew the portières back. A column of flame leaped up in the hall, blotting out all three men there.

"*Quick!*" Adair ran forward, dropped his gun, shielded his face with an arm as he went to his knees. He stuck out a hand, dragged in someone. It was the attendant. Desher and Jeremy shoved him aside, groped in the seething flames. They touched something on the floor, grabbed, yanked it in.

It was the little brown man. The man with the cape—Kokamori.

The flames roared higher, licked into the foyer. Jeremy stood and kicked the door shut. "Let that yellow devil roast," he said.

"God, my hands!" Desher said softly. "They're pretty badly burned." But he looked around calmly, asked, "What do you do for a fire alarm here?"

"We do without one," Adair said grimly. "The doors and walls are fireproofed. The only thing that can burn outside is the rug, the two chairs, the table and the lamp that's on it."

*"And* that stocky yellow man," the F.B.I. man reminded him.

"Let him burn," Adair snarled. "Any man who pays a call on me with a drawn gun has to take his own chances!"

Desher shook his head, still dazed by Adair's changed manner. But as he started for the living room he smiled slightly, "You never know!"

Then Desher snapped on the lights. "If you don't mind, Cary, we won't call any help yet. This is a government affair, now. I recognized one of those men out in the hall."

Adair's voice had a tinge of relief. "All right, Jo. You, Jeremy—give me a hand with these chaps."

Kokamori and the attendant were carried into the room. Both were stunned and slightly, though painfully, burned. Desher came close to the little brown man, leaned over him. A grim smile twisted the G-man's mouth.

"Ah! Captain Kokamori! So we've finally caught up with you?"

Adair looked. "You know him?"

"You bet I know him. He's a Japanese naval spy!" He swung to the man again. "Who is the chap who burned to death, out there?"

Kokamori's eyes blinked shut; then opened slowly again. "Pliss. I do not know. I verre sorry."

The Government agent stared at the attendant. "Who's that man?"

Adair stepped over and looked at the man. The hall man was moaning and holding his head. "He's one of my men," he identified him. "That is, he works in the building. He's all right—I *think*."

Jeremy bent his head a moment, then walked to the foyer. He said, "I don't hear the sound of the fire here, Mr. Adair! Can it have gone out?"

Adair stepped to the wall, clicked a switch. Desher stooped and frisked the two men on the floor. "I don't trust anybody," he growled. But the men were unarmed.

The F.B.I. man straightened, peered out into the foyer hall. The servant, Jeremy, was struggling with the knob, the switch not working. Adair went through to help him, gave the handle a twist and a jerk. The door swung open. Smoke eddied into the foyer from the rug that had been burned to a crisp. And the light had been burned out. Jeremy snapped the side-lights on, carried across a portable lamp with a long cord. He tilted it over, pointed it into the hall.

*"Well, I'll be*—er—Mr. Adair, sir?" Jeremy's calm returned. Cary and Desher crossed over, after a searching look at the two men in the living room.

"What is it, Jeremy? Is he—is he that badly burned?"

Jeremy shook his head slowly. "There's no one here to be burned, sir. The husky, yellow man has—disappeared! The elevator door is shut and the car gone, also. There are just the burned rug, the chairs, lamp, table, and—" The servant paused, stepped into the blackened hall.

He leaned over, picked something off the floor. "And this!"

He passed the thing he had found to Adair and Desher. It was a black oblong of paper… with the blood-red salamander and the signature—

Desher said, *"The Emperor of the Dead!"* in an awed voice.

From the room behind them came the sudden, sibilant hiss of the Japanese naval spy.

## CHAPTER 4
## HELLBENT FOR TROUBLE

JO DESHER returned to the center of the living room, his hands wrapped in oil-saturated cloths. Before him were the attendant and the man called Kokamori.

Adair and Jeremy stood behind him, their eyes alert. But they were silent. Desher swung to the badly frightened attendant.

"You understand that you are to keep your mouth shut about

what went on here, to-day? When you go home, stay in the house. I'm going to check on you!"

Adair said quietly. "He'll keep shut." He turned to the man. "I can arrange for two weeks vacation, with pay and all medical expenses, *and* a bonus—If you shut up about this. It's government business, you understand?"

"I'll shut up, Mr. Adair."

Kokamori was staring keenly at Adair. "Pliss—who are you?"

"Nobody much," was the calm answer. "I own this building, though. And I can do pretty much what I want with it and with anyone who works here."

The little naval spy was smiling again. "Hard to understand," he said genially. "Building owner has spy traps, uses many guns when men come near."

Desher said derisively, "They came in sort of handy to-day, Kokamori." But his eyes were puzzled, agreeing, almost, with the spy's words. "Cary—how about letting your hall man go now? I have some things I want to ask Kokamori."

Adair motioned to the man. "Jeremy will look after the doctors and the pay," he said. "But if so much as one word is said about this—*one word, mind you!*—you're out of a job."

"And into the government clink," Desher threatened him.

When the man had left, the Federal agent turned to the Japanese officer. "Well? I'm waiting. What were you doing tracking me? What were you doing in the hallway with that gunman? Who was that chap with you? Eh?"

"Pliss, I do not know anything." He smiled disarmingly, but it didn't go over with Desher.

30

"What caused that explosion in the hall?" he demanded.

"Pliss! I do not know." The man's eyes turned to Adair again, busy as a little animal. "You rich; you owner of building; you do no work. But—you have spy traps and you shoot so straight with gun."

"Forget him, Kokamori. Listen to me. Just who is the Emperor of the Dead?"

The little brown man's eyes wavered and fell. "I—do not know," he whispered. "I—never hear such name before."

"You lie like hell," Desher thrust the paper at him—the paper with the salamander and the blood-red signature. "Ever see that before?" The man's head came up. He licked his lips nervously.

"Is the Emperor of the Dead another name for your emperor? For the Emperor of Japan?" Desher wanted to know.

The spy came to his feet. "The Mikado is emperor of *life*, not of death. He is direct descendant of sun god. Sun rises on Japanese flag, in token of rising sun god. Mikado not Emperor of the Dead."

Desher looked at him keenly. "Don't kid me, Kokamori. One of *our* navy men, Jerry Hammager, was wiped out by the Emperor of the Dead—one month ago. We both know that. Come on, *talk!*"

"Pliss... I know nothing."

"Okay," Desher growled. "Maybe the sun rises on your flag, but you're not rising with it! You're one rising *son* that's going to set—and you'll set on your pants in a coop until you're ready to talk turkey."

31

Three guns ripped lead and the
foyer was consumed with flames.

"Pliss. I have no affairs to do with Turkey."
"Aw, dry up!" Desher turned to Adair and Jeremy.

"I'd like to have a little private confab with you two," he said quietly. "I'll handcuff my setting sun, here, and we'll talk in another room!"

**THE EMPEROR** of the Dead came through a narrow, arched passage in the rockwall and into the flaring lights of the torches. He nodded abruptly to the *salaams* of the grotesquely muscular and dwarfed hunchback, Bikko.

"You have news for me?"

"Yes, sire. Marku telephoned, from New York," answered Bikko.

"The message?"

"Marku met with the-man-of-the-iron-boats, whilst following the American detective. He was listening at the door of the friend of the detective, when a trap was sprung."

The ascetic, saintly face of the Emperor of the Dead went hard. "What sort of trap? How?"

"Marku knows not, sire—other than that a door was sprung open and many men fired at him."

The emperor's face was alert, keen. "Who is this friend of the detective?"

"One Adair, so he styles himself, sire. He is a rich man who toils not." The man paused to poke the mat of glowing coals higher in flame. "Marku was wounded, the cleansing fire was exploded."

"Exploded? The cleansing fire? Then the American detective was *cleansed?* And the man-of-the-iron-boats?"

Bikko cringed before he spoke. "The man-of-the-iron-boats,

yes; and one other, a laborer in the building, sire. But the American detective and his friends were not cleansed by the fire."

The Emperor of the Dead came close, his face a mask of rage. "Marku is a bungler!" he rasped. He stood before the cringing man a moment, then: "This friend of the American detective, this rich man who toils not—*yet has spy traps!*"

His voice had dropped to a low whisper.

There was a moment of silence, while the torches of the frigid dungeon flickered their flame over that severe, forbidding face. The coals in the mat of fire glowed brightly. The Emperor of the Dead passed a pink tongue over his thin, drawn lips.

"Marku is to investigate this friend who toils not, yet has spy traps! He is again to pursue the American detective! The Emperor of the Dead so orders!"

"But, sire—Marku, he is wounded, is painfully burned."

*"Marku shall be further burned if he fails!"*

"But he says he cannot move, sire."

"Marku *shall* move." The voice was low, brutal. "He shall move though the devils of torment eat him, body and soul. He shall move with those other subjects of the Emperor of the Dead who are near him, and cleanse the American detective—*and his friend, who toils not!*"

Bikko shivered; but it was not because of the frigid air of the place. The Emperor of the Dead chanted a deep monotone, swayed to the bed of coals, mounted his bare feet into them and slowly walked through.

Still swaying and chanting, he made his way to the narrow

arch in the rocks, paused a moment, his yellowish-white body standing stark against the black stones.

"The Emperor of the Dead cleanses all with fire, takes charge of the souls of those so cleansed." The hollow voice rang loud in the cavern.

"It is so, sire!"

Bikko *salaamed* low and went to the niche where the telephone was hidden.

DESHER STOOD in the pantry of Cary Adair's penthouse. The door to the living room was shut. He had handcuffed Kokamori and left him sitting in the big chair in the outer room. He turned to Adair.

"What's back of this secret alarm business?" he asked Adair quietly. "And how is it that you and Jeremy are armed to the teeth? What are you so—*afraid* of?"

"Well, Jo," Adair said, speaking slowly. "I seem to remember that someone tried to kill us here, a while back, when you were calling. A chap who was impersonating one of your own men, I believe?" At Desher's nod, he went on. "Furthermore, I keep quite a bit of money and valuable antiques, rare books and manuscripts, other worthwhile *objets d'art* in this apartment."

"Nuts," Desher snapped. "You're not the only man who has valuables to protect. Why not leave it to the cops?"

"Down here, at *night?* You forget how isolated this place is, Jo."

Desher grunted. "But this isn't night. It's broad daylight."

Adair sighed. "Am I supposed to regulate the time when hijackers try to hit me? Anyway," he smiled slightly, "you're the one responsible for this visit. Laugh that one off."

Desher considered. "You got pistol permits, both of you?"

The servant produced one from a small case he carried in his pocket, made

out to *Jeremy Watkyns*, before the G-man had even finished his question. Adair obliged, too; but his manner was cold.

"I'm sorry, Cary," Desher said, after a moment. "It—just struck me as being odd, you know. That alarm, and the door-trap; and the way you chaps went for your gats, was—well, I didn't know you had it in you!"

Adair dropped his eyes. "Spur-of-the-moment action, Jo. Instinctive, I imagine. Rather surprised myself, y'know." His voice contrived a touch of injury, of sadness. "But—to have you question me as though I were a—er—suspicious character, a—er—*racketeer!* That's a bit thick, old man."

"Aw, forget it, Cary. I'll be back when this case is wound up and we'll have a nice little get-together. Right now, I'm taking my friend Kokamori to Washington and see if I can't make him squeak a bit. He'll catch hell in his own country because of this."

The Federal man rubbed his hands together in pleasure at

his capture, and stepped past Adair and Jeremy to swing the pantry door open. He stepped into the living room—and gasped.

*"My God! Kokamori's gone!"*

Adair frowned. He pushed by Jeremy and helped Desher search the penthouse thoroughly. Jeremy disappeared, came back in a moment.

"Mr. Adair, sir—the guest bedroom! The bedclothes have been pulled from the bed, knotted, and are hanging down from the window!"

Adair jumped to the house telephone. He got a hall-man. "Block all elevators!" he snapped. "A Japanese—er—" he looked at Desher, got his negative shake of the head—"a little Japanese," he went on, "was caught in my apartment. I had him handcuffed, but he got away to another floor. Down a sheet-rope he tossed out the window...."

Adair listened a moment, then dropped the receiver back on the hook. "He's gone," he said, his eyes hard. "The hall-man says a woman secretary working on the sixty-second floor fell in a faint when a man climbed into the open window by her desk. But she revived a bit too late. A man of Kokamori's de-scription was seen leaving the building!"

Desher was incredulous. "Wearing handcuffs?"

Adair nodded. "Unless he was able to shed them in some way." He looked up quickly. "Couldn't he hide his hands under his cape?"

"Yeah," Desher growled, his face drawn. "My God—I'll catch it for this job!"

Adair's face was sympathetic. "Can't you keep it to yourself until you can get a new line on him?"

"Hell, no! I'm a Government agent—not a damned coward. The important thing isn't my job—it's getting Kokamori!" He walked to the outside telephone, raised it, called a number.

"Inspector Desher speaking," he clipped. "Ishii Kokamori, Japanese operative, was captured by me in an attempt on my life. He—" the man faltered, forced himself on. "He escaped a short time ago. I'm on my way to the Bureau to file the report. Post the alarm, and watch all outgoing trains, steamships and roads. We'll check his haunts as soon as I get there." He banged down the 'phone.

He pushed Jeremy back impatiently when the servant held out his coat. He didn't notice the 'Emperor of the Dead' paper, with the salamander and the scrawled signature, that he had left on the small table.

"I'll be in touch with you when this thing is off my chest," he barked, as he went out.

Adair turned to his servant. "Think the heat ruined our camera?"

Jeremy frowned his concern and went quickly into the hall. He stared at one of the tiles in the wall. "The lens is cracked, sir—but maybe—"

He came into the foyer again, opened a secret panel and stepped into a narrow recess. A light flashed on, showing an automatic moving-picture film machine positioned against the wall—a camera with its lens trained through one of the tiles of the hall outside.

"The alarm system is burned out, sir," Jeremy said, after a moment. "When the men stood here, on the rug, they touched off the electric switch and started the machine—but the fire destroyed it."

"And the film?"

Jeremy snapped the box open, reached in his hand. His face was glowing when he turned.

"No, Mr. Adair. The film is intact—and run off!"

"Develop it," Adair snapped. "I'd like to see what was going on there—and how that man escaped—Kokamori's companion."

In the darkened living room, Adair sat quietly and watched a strange drama unfold on the miniature movie screen in front of him.

…A husky, yellow skinned man backed slowly from the elevator door. Following him, hands high in the air, was Ishii Kokamori.

Adair swarmed to his feet. "My God, Jeremy! That wasn't the way Desher figured it. Look. *Look!* The yellow man is *covering* Kokamori!"

Jeremy whispered, "Yes, sir. I believe you are right!"

"Then—the Emperor of the Dead hasn't anything to do with the Japanese."

"Why, sir? Isn't that yellow man a Jap?"

"Looks more like a breed, Jeremy," Adair said. "A mixture of races."

The film unwound, showing the trio edging nearer the door. The cream-colored cylinder was in clearer view. And so was the yellow man's face, as it menaced Kokamori. Adair clipped:

"We're right, Jeremy! That yellow man is covering both the hallman *and* the Japanese spy!" He said, "Take it easy, now! Watch the floor for that Emperor of the Dead note! Watch to see who drops it."

But Kokamori and the hallman remained rigidly quiet with the yellow man's gun threatening them; and the gunman was poised close to the door in a listening attitude.

"What do you make of that cylinder, Jeremy?"

"Can't fathom it, sir. But I'd swear that's what started the fire and the explosion. A bomb, probably?"

Adair grunted. "Maybe." But he was quiet as the battle scene flashed on. The film kept unwinding the drama, then there was a flash, and a curtain of flame shot across the screen, blotting out everything with inky smoke.

Then, the fire died a bit, sagged to show the walls, flickered. The hall came into full view and only a small spot of flame remained. Completely, the fire died. Only the smoking embers that had been chairs and a table, and a crisp, curled, charred remnant of the rug remained.

That, and in the middle of the scorched white tiling of the floor a square of black—the sign and the signature of the Emperor of the Dead!

Darkness had fallen. Adair sat in an easy chair, his face thoughtful. "Try to get Mr. Desher again, Jeremy."

"Yes, sir." The servant went to the telephone, called F.B.I. headquarters in New York. After a brief conversation, he put the instrument down and came into the living room.

"Mr. Desher is away on important, secret business, sir. He can't be reached for several weeks at least, sir."

"You gave my message. Urgent business?"

"I did, sir." The man shrugged. "But F.B.I. says that they are trying to reach him, also. They seemed anxious."

"My God!" Cary Adair came to his feet. "Jeremy, he should be there by now, easily. Maybe—?" He paused, his eyes completing the question. The servant nodded gloomily.

"I'm—er—I'm afraid maybe you're right, sir. Either the Emperor of the Dead, or Mr. Kokamori, I'd say, could tell us his whereabouts."

Adair's face was white. "But—the F.B.I. has got to know this story! They've got to know what *we* know! That the Emperor of the Dead may not be—well, what they think it is."

"Show them this film, sir?"

An ironic smile crossed Adair's features. "You're forgetting something, aren't you? That we have nothing to back up the story with? If Desher is gone, if anything has happened to him—that implicates us!"

"Oh. Yes, sir. It might be—er—embarrassing."

Adair's face wrinkled in a frown. He snapped his fingers. "The hallman! Jeremy, *he* must know if that man was threatening Kokamori. That will back up our story. Otherwise, the F.B.I. might just as well as not take us into camp on this affair."

"Mr. Desher could clear us, when he came back, sir."

Adair's face was taut. "And if he *doesn't* come back?"

"Oh."

"Call the manager's office of the building," Adair ordered.

"Get the name of the man who was burned, and his address. We'll go to his home and question him about the thing. Then, if we must, we'll go to the F.B.I. with him."

Jeremy was back in two minutes, his face grave, his eyes blazing. "I called, sir."

"Well?" Adair started suddenly. He gripped Jeremy's shoulders, shook him. "Speak up, man! What is it?"

"There was a bad fire, sir—at that man's apartment. Just an hour ago. The manager's office received word, just before I called. *The hallman is dead... burned to death!*"

Adair sighed. "...Houses that burn in the night... Comets that flash over them... Navy spies... G-men... Extortion... Helium gas... Cylinders that burn and leave *unburned* notes behind... Salamanders... *And The Emperor of the Dead!*"

Pin-points of excitement showed in Adair's eyes. He took a deep breath. "Orders, Jeremy!"

Notebook and pencil jumped into the gaunt man's hands. "Yes, sir?"

"Notify the building office we'll be away for a short time. Next—*money*. Next—"

HANDSOME, FASHIONABLY-DRESSED Cary Adair stepped lightly from his private elevator into the deserted hall of the great office building. He nodded genially to the night man on duty. Behind Adair came gaunt, severe Jeremy, his frame swaying with the weight of the two suitcases he carried.

The watchman looked up. "Going away, Mr. Adair?"

"I need a bit of rest. That fire upstairs to-day, you know."

"Yes. I heard! Short circuit, wasn't it?"

Adair smiled lazily. "That describes it to perfection. 'A short-circuit that nobody knows anything about!'"

The man blinked. "But—they know about it now, don't they? About the short-circuit?"

"Several people do," Adair agreed, as he swept on.

The watchman shook his head. "Queer cuss," he muttered.

Jeremy put the bags down on the sidewalk outside and waved a taxi over to the curb. Adair climbed in, with Jeremy after him.

"Drive," the servant told the cabby.

"Huh? Drive? Where to?"

"I'll tell you that as you go along. Just—*drive!*"

Adair stared out the window for some minutes as the cab went north on Broadway. Then he turned. "You got good prints?"

"Yes, sir."

The two lapsed into silence as the cab bowled north to Fourteenth Street. Then, Jeremy called, "Turn to the right." The driver swung his wheel and headed east.

But neither Adair nor Jeremy noticed the small, black car that tagged in their wake by several blocks, making turn for turn as they went along the darkened streets.

## CHAPTER 5
## WHARF WAR

SOMEWHERE IN the distance, a bell sounded mournfully, twice. A junkman's truck clattered noisily over the cobbles of South Street, along the East River. A scrawny black cat looked up from where it was balanced atop a battered garbage tin. Something was moving in the shadows of the building line.

The cat arched its back stiffly, and hissed. The shadows loosed two wraiths that scuttled nearer, making the prowling feline's hair rise in a ruff of anger—or fear. It jumped to the sidewalk and fled into the doorway of a darkened flat.

The wraiths materialized into two masked men who paused, stooped over low, looked up and down the street. Rapidly, they sped across the gloomy old pier, were swallowed up in the dark of the place. A light flashed briefly, then died again.

Two masked men paused, looked up and down the street. Captain Satan said, "Come on, Slim. Soapy will be expecting us. Don't forget your call letters or you're apt to get a belly full of lead."

"Right, Captain."

A watchful man stood in the partly opened door of the wharf as Satan and his lieutenant approached.

"You're covered!" his husky voice broke into the stillness.

"S-M," Satan's lieutenant replied and ghosted inside the door.

There was a chuckle. "And who is the other, Slim?"

The other man spoke for himself. "Captain Satan," he said, then, "Glad to see you Soapy, are the other boys here?"

"Sure thing, Cap'n. They're waiting inside."

Satan paused. He said, "I have a hunch, boys. I think there's going to be a little action."

"What do you mean, Captain?" Slim demanded.

"Across the street there," Satan directed. "That dark shadow. It's moving, and I think I know what it is."

45

"Damned if I do," said Slim.

"Never mind that," Satan told him. He turned to the other man. "Soapy, go back and tell the rest of the gang to lie low. Slim! Give me that tommy-gun."

His lieutenant swiftly complied, and Satan gripped the gun

in his hands. "Our Oriental pals are not as smart as they suppose," Satan cracked sharply. The shadow across the street advanced slowly. It looked like a dark, moving blanket. "The fools!" Satan observed. "They can't get away with this."

He tossed a coin at the opposite wall. From under that strange blanket there blazed forth the red blast of a gun. The shot pinged harmlessly into the wood. Satan told Slim tensely, "Let 'em have your artillery!"

Slim let loose with his two automatics at the same moment Satan's tommy-gun bit through the night. The blanket had advanced swiftly, rushed inside the wharf. Satan's tommy-gun swept through it without mercy, and in the dim light they could see it collapse. Perhaps a half dozen dead men lay beneath the blanket.

Satan's gun had stopped its deadly chatter. The swift beat of running feet could be heard in the heavy silence. "One of them got away," Satan said. "Must have lost his guts and made a break."

"Lemme knock him over," Slim requested.

"No, hold your fire, Slim. We can use that guy to throw the cops off the trail."

Even as he spoke, the shrill shriek of a police siren came to their ears. Satan and Slim withdrew into the darkness. A car without any lights sped through the gloom. Satan said, "The fool is trying to make a getaway in that car. Now watch the cops go after him. They won't even know we're alive."

The police siren grew louder. A police car careened around a corner on two wheels and Satan could hear a copper shouting, "There he goes. Dead ahead of us. Step on it, Mike!"

Satan pushed the door of the place shut, stood looming large and broad in the half-light cast by the lamp that glowed up onto the ceiling. In a semi-circle around him stood a half-score of masked men, guns in their hands. One, taller than any of the others, and clad in severe black, held a machine gun in his hand.

"You're all right, Captain?"

"Yes, Slim. Get that stand-lamp and train it on this blanket here by the door. This trick is used in the Orient, just as the Indians in this country used to sneak up on unwary pioneers with branches as camouflage."

Slim brought the lamp down to the floor. The bulging gray

blanket was ripped by half a thousand slugs. One of Satan's men gasped. But Satan's voice was calm. "Pull that blanket aside, Slim. I imagine they're all dead."

Satan's lieutenant leaned over and reached with his long, sensitive fingers. He yanked; and a murmur came from the others of the crew. A group of six huddled forms lay there in the light, soaking in a great pool of dark red blood.

A strong flashlight sprang alive in Satan's hand. He motioned to one of the men, trained the flash on those still forms. As the bodies were turned one by one, Satan played his flash on the dead features. Before the light had even jumped away, another of the crew was methodically going through the dead man's pockets.

Satan's light fell on the last of the six corpses. He exclaimed, "Slim! Look who's here! I had a hunch we'd meet again."
SATAN'S LIEUTENANT stooped, stared into a wide, flat, yellow face that was blistered with recently-acquired burns. A long sigh escaped Satan.

"The Emperor of the Dead has lost some valued subjects," he said soberly. "Doc?" A slender, stooped figure came into the light.

"Yes, Cap'n."

"Check those men, to see if they're dead. If they are, the boys will roll them into the river—weighted down, of course. But I want fingerprints of them all. Also, strip them to the skin and examine the bodies for identifying scars. Who are the best men to help you, Doc?"

The little man considered. "Kayo and Gentleman Dan."

"You heard," Satan spoke. He swung to Slim. "You got them all checked, Slim? The crew?"

"Right, Captain. All our boys have been checked. They're okay." He paused, adjusted the mask on his long, lean face. "But I can't understand how that one guy got loose and escaped."

Satan's voice was grim. "Wherever he goes, the news will go with him to his master: that Satan and his crew are out to give the phony Emperor of the Dead a damned good punch in the nose. But let's finish the job here and get on with the meeting."

Five minutes later, the six corpses plopped into the dreary waters of the East River.

Satan called the meeting together. Only the flickering light of the lamp broke the gloom. A tight mask of black silk covered the upper half of his strong and chiseled features. His broad shoulders and muscular back were set off by the tight and severe black jacket he wore. His strong hands and muscular wrists were powerful even in repose.

He passed a hand over his closely-cropped hair. His mouth was wide, strong. Beside him, his somber eyes alert on the masked men who crouched low on the floor, was Slim.

"Pay close attention, men," Satan said at length, in a low, clear voice.

"Yes, Cap'n," the answer came—from all but one man. That member, a slender, weazened individual with a hawk nose, said:

"Yes, Captain. Sure. We're listening."

Satan's eyes narrowed. "Who are you? What are your call letters? Your emergency letters?"

"I'm Solly," the hawk-nosed one said, his voice trembling.

49

"My letters are S-L. Remember? They should be 'S-Y,' but you changed 'em because Soapy's were like that, too. Remember?"

"That's Solly, Captain," Slim said softly. "There's no mistake about that."

"I remember, Solly," Satan said drily. "But—suppose *you* remember that the only man in this group who calls me 'Captain' is Slim! The rest of you call me 'Cap'n.'"

"Oi, I forgot, Cap'n," Solly said contritely.

"Masked men can't afford to have poor memories, Solly. When identification must be quick and positive, a slip of the memory may mean *death!*" He looked over at the little man who had examined the bodies.

"Find anything important, Doc?"

"Yes and no, Cap'n. Those men were Orientals, all of them. Japanese, unless I'm greatly mistaken. A *mixture* of Japanese blood, certainly." At a nod of agreement from Satan, he gestured with his small, capable looking hands. "So I was not surprised to find knife wounds on every one of them, but their feet had me puzzled."

The entire group started. Satan frowned. "Their feet were strange? Deformed? What do you mean?"

"No, Cap'n," Doc said. "Not deformed in any way. But the soles of their feet are strangely hardened, the skin and flesh have become almost like plaster." He turned to a tall, debonaire man with a waxed mustache and black, patent-leather hair. "How did it strike you, Gentleman Dan?"

"I rapped the soles of one dead man's feet with the butt of my gun. It cracked loud as a skull!" Dan said.

Several members of the crew laughed. But Satan's face was lighted up with interest. "Think carefully, Doc! Were they *thick-soles?* Like elephant-hide, almost?"

"That's right, Cap'n." The little doctor cocked his head, thought. "It was as if their feet had been *baked* hard, by—well, the way a hot sidewalk would do to your feet, for instance, if you walked on it bare-footed for a long time."

Satan stood with his head bent. He seemed to be considering. But, finally, he shook his head slowly. "No. It can't be. It doesn't fit. Not... *that*—and extortion." He looked up. "Identification on any of them? Names? Anything important?"

Kayo pointed to a pile of nondescript pencils, pens, handkerchiefs, unmarked keys— automatics, ammunition clips, knives... and a long, fat envelope. He bent over.

"I got this from a stiff with burn-marks on him. It's stuffed with dough." He passed it to Slim. The crew lieutenant opened it, his eyes widening, and counted quickly.

"This mob is well heeled. Captain," he said slowly. "Twenty grand in this envelope."

"Identify the money," Satan snapped. "Check the bills."

Slim shook his head. "Small bills," he said. "And old, worn ones, too."

Excitement shone in Satan's face. "So it's big game we're after, eh? Well—we can use it!" A grim smile played over his face.

A whistle from outside cut in on him, a low, soft whistle. Slim said to Kayo: "Take Soapy's post. He wants to tell us something."

In a moment, the furtive little man stuck his head inside, his pale eyes blinking against the light.

"I found sumpin' in th' street, outside th' door, Slim. It maybe ain't anything important. A container, sort of; creamy-colored an' light." The man stuck his hand in.

"Here, Slim—*catch!*"

An expression of horror passed over Satan's face when he saw the thing—a cream-colored cylinder of some sort of transparent material, of about two-quart size.

Slim gasped "Oh, my God! Jump for your lives, everyone!" He tried to step forward to catch the thing that was floating, more than dropping, toward him.

But he couldn't move a muscle, he stood in paralyzed stupor as the thing floated down slowly toward the wharf floor.

# CHAPTER 6
# TWO CLUES

THE HUNCHBACK Bikko cringed before the Emperor of the Dead. "It is not I who has done the bungling, sire," he mumbled, bowing his head repeatedly. "I only repeat the words of Sanso."

The Emperor said, "Repeat again, Foul One, the words of that knave who styles himself Sanso. Repeat—and slowly!"

"The Rich One was followed when he left the great building, sire," Bikko explained. "He went by motor to a beggars' section of New York, and there into an alley. Sanso assembled many of your subjects, sire, and they waited. In time the Rich One reappeared, but this time differently garbed. The Rich One was a poorer and larger one now, and had over his face a masking of black. He was followed by his slave, who was dressed the same."

"Hold!" The Emperor of the Dead considered, stroking his sensitive chin with long, well manicured fingers. "He went by automobile—to a poor section of the city. Yes! Yes! He changed clothes, masked himself." He swung to the dwarf again. "Continue, Foul One!"

Bikko stared fixedly at one of the flares as he continued his recital of the telephone report that had come to him. "Into a covered wharf went the Rich One and his slave. Sanso, Marku and five others followed, shrouded in a curtain that was the same as the night above them. They entered into the wharf—"

Bikko's face became agitated, his thick lips writhing back from the blackened stumps of his teeth. "…And scarcely were Sanso, Marku and the others in this wharf than a noise occurred, such as would be made by a man who stumbles and falls into a wall. The subjects of the Emperor of the Dead fired their flame-weapons at the sound. But a great gun spoke to them from another direction, killing outright six of the subjects of the Emperor. Sanso escaped—and Sanso alone."

"Bungling fools," the emperor growled. "And what of the fire that was to cleanse these impure ones? What of the golden fortune with which Marku had been intrusted?"

"The fire that was to cleanse was not used," Bikko said, blinking his little black eyes at the flare. "The golden fortune remained with the corpse of your subject, Marku."

The Emperor of the Dead screamed imprecations and swayed from side to side as he tottered in a circle around the cringing Bikko. "My fortune!" he screamed. "May Marku's soul roast on the spit of the Devil himself!" He paused, aware that Bikko's eyes had swung to him.

"Not, Bikko, that it is the gold I value! Nay! Gold and the love of it is the curse of the world, and I, Emperor of the Dead, have no use for it, other than to cleanse the impure. I cleanse the impure by removing the gold they love, and cleansing them with a pure fire, bring them to The Emperor of the Dead—The Empire of the Dead, where gold has no use, no meaning!"

Yet his eyes flamed madly, despite his protestations.

But Bikko apparently had not noticed the fury of his sire, at mention of the loss of the money. He was adding a point to his narrative.

"Bikko knows the sire's hatred of gold," he whined. "But it is that other—that mention you made of Marku. What did you say, sire?"

"Ah! I said, 'May his soul roast on the spit of the Devil himself.'"

Bikko nodded his head up and down happily. "The wish of the sire is already granted," said Bikko. "Sanso has reported that a great light appeared over his head, shining on the ceiling of the wharf. It was a strange light, formed in a circle, sire. And in the center of the circle appeared the Devil himself, a sharp fork of great size threatening them all!"

The Emperor stared, passed his hand over his eyes. "What? What is this nonsense that you speak, Bikko? The Devil himself appeared?" He chuckled low, shook his head. "It is the story of a lying dog!"

"But, sire"—Bikko spread his knotted hands—"it is Sanso himself who has said it. I am not saying wrong, sire? Sanso said the Satan who appeared—"

"Stop!" The Emperor of the Dead stumbled, put out a hand for support. Bikko jumped to his aid. The dwarf led the tottering, saintly-faced man to the throne, helped him up to it. He retired with many *salaams,* watched him covertly.

*"Satan!"* the Emperor of the Dead whispered, his eyes stricken. "I am so near the goal—and then—*Satan!"*

He sat in thought for some time, then stirred. He beckoned Bikko. He was calm again; but his eyes were thoughtful, busy, and a fanatical gleam shone in them.

"The forces of evil, of the impure, are great around me! Listen, carefully, Bikko—and give my orders to Sanso: First—the American detective is to be liberated; I shall not cleanse him—*yet.*

"Next: The man-of-the-iron-boats is to be liberated. But let the American detective hear mention of a certain place known as Thatcher, Colorado. You understand? And let the man-of-the-iron-boats hear mention of secret activity at that same spot." He paused. "Repeat!"

Bikko repeated the orders in a high monotone. The Emperor of the Dead gave approval, and added, "Sanso shall then insert in the newspapers of New York a certain advertisement, offering a rich reward for the return of a certain object. Describe the object thus:—*One cream-colored container, lost on the night of—*" He paused. "Mention no date, Bikko! *Just say, Reward of One Thousand Dollars for return of—*"

**JO DESHER** lay on the crude mattress in the deserted warehouse, dimly awake. His head was splitting with pain. He blinked his eyes in the poor light, stared at the high ceiling above him.

The sound of voices came from an adjoining room—voices that were high-pitched, sing-song. After a moment, he was able to reconstruct things.

"Let's see," he remembered. "I left Cary Adair's and checked in to the New York Bureau. A 'phone call tipped me to a place down on the East Side...."

His sore brain followed his steps from there. First, a drab, Oriental restaurant—the sandwich and the coffee—bitter coffee—that he drank while he was waiting for his 'tipster.' But he could think no further.

"That coffee," he swore. "Wait till I get out of here, and I'll fix *that* joint! They must have loaded that Java with knockout drops!" But a rueful smile came over his face a moment later. "If I *ever* get out alive!"

He stilled, listening to the voices in the next room. Half-heartedly, he strained at the bonds that bound his hands behind his back. He choked back a gasp when he found them slipping, slightly. But he quieted again. He was all-ears for that conversation in the next room.

"...In two nights," he heard that singsong voice say in English, "we shall break the great wells at Thatcher; and then it is done."

"Thatcher?" another voice asked. "You mean, Colorado? Ah,

yes! The helium wells shall be destroyed, crippling them for immediate use. It is the machinery that is important, is it not? The machinery to extract the helium? And then, with our immense supplies, we shall be in a position to bomb America, and she cannot defend!"

"Silence!" that other voice said. "The American detective!"

"Ha!" There was a chuckle. "What matter of him? When we leave, he remains—securely tied. If he lives four or five days, without food or water, he might be found. But by then the damage shall be done, the victory ours."

There was a scraping of chairs, the sound of footsteps on the bare floor, and the light was turned out. A door slammed a moment later, a key rattled in the lock.

Grimly, Desher wrestled with his bonds.

ISHII KOKAMORI had already consigned his soul to his ancestors. He sat rigidly erect in the chair, bound hand and foot. He had been imprisoned more than twelve hours, now. And for some hours before that, unconscious as the result of a blow over the head. Now he was awake, although his head throbbed in torture.

"The restaurant," he sighed. "Ah, yes! It was foolhardy of me to venture alone. I should have informed one of my men."

His eyes were sad as they rested on the candle that lighted the room. It was on a table, seven feet away. But in that next room sat those others—those fanatical cut-throats—listening for the slightest sound.

They were talking now...

"...The gas already stored at Thatcher—that is in Colorado—is to be seized. Then the machinery. Oh, it is of great weight, yes. But what of that, with the master having already taken that fact into his plans!"

"It will succeed, then?" The other voice was tense with interest.

Kokamori's eyes flamed with interest; but saddened again. He could not get to that table, to burn the bonds that tied him to the chair, without those others hearing. He shrugged.

"I shall never escape to be there," he thought. "Of what use to outwit Desher, when I fall into such an awkward trap!" His mind slid to Cary Adair, and he frowned as he considered the man.

"Odd, that one," he murmured. "Such eyes; but so obviously a rich idler. And yet—"

His mind jerked away from that subject as he heard the conversation from the next room.

"…Let us go out and eat! Is it not time for that? My stomach is sobbing bitterly."

"But—Kokamori?"

*"Pfut.* He is trussed like a bird! We can eat our fill, return when we wish. Come."

"We come," the other voices answered.

Kokamori sat in stunned silence, scarcely breathing, as feet scraped in that other room and the light was dimmed. The slam of a door left him suspicious, however. He smiled foxily, his eyes on the door.

"There is such a thing as too much fortune!" he thought.

He counted to a thousand, listening intently. A rat was

scurrying in the wall behind him. He counted another hundred, then moved in his chair, noisily.

Still no sound from that other room.

Cautiously, Kokamori shoved his weight forward, got awkwardly to his feet. He was hunched over uncomfortably, but after a pause, he shuffled as silently as he could toward that table where the candle burned.

The flame seared his hands cruelly when he backed the chair to the candle, seared the hands that had already been burned that day. But Ishii Kokamori hissed through his teeth and bore it....

## CHAPTER 7
## THE LONG ROAD TO HELL

THE CREW in the pier sat in stunned silence at Slim's words... and his obvious fright. They watched the cream-colored cylinder sail slowly to the floor, making a half turn as it dropped.

Satan stepped a pace forward, trapped the thing in his hands and gave with it, to reduce the shock. Slim emitted a shuddering sigh and wiped the beads of perspiration from his face with a long, trembling hand.

"The next time you throw anything, Soapy," Satan said gently, "I'll throw you. And you won't sail as lightly as this explosive did, either!"

"Explosive!"

"Something like that," Satan told them mildly. He signaled

59

a big, florid-faced, blond man. "Dutchman? You're somewhat of a chemist, aren't you? Have a look at this and see what you think it is—the outer part!" He passed it to the man carefully.

"And you can all listen to the story," he told the men, and started with his tale. When he had concluded, he said:

"The F.B.I. is in this. The Japanese Navy is in it. And some other group. You had a look at the third outfit, just to-night. What it is, who it is, why it is—I don't know. We're not bucking the Federal Bureau of Investigation, men. I don't fight the Law. I fight alongside of—or ahead of—the Law.

"I have no quarrel with F.B.I. methods. They're fine. But you know my principles: I'll smash every crook I can lay my hands on—and what he has is mine! I'll break every petty or large crook, every swindling racketeer or grafting politician or gyp banker I can lay my hands on.

"The terms you already know. What they have is ours. I pay the expenses and take a one-third cut. You boys split the remainder on equal shares. Some of you have been working with me long enough to be independently wealthy. You could retire. But, like me, you are men for whom the ordinary pace of life is not geared high enough. We want something more—more action—more excitement." He paused, smiled. "Of course, we don't pass up any material gains that may come along. And up to now, the take has been satisfactory!"

"Oi, and how!" Solly murmured.

"Shut up," Satan snapped. "Slim has some orders to give you lads. Listen closely—do your jobs thoroughly and quickly. Get back to our next appointed meeting place *exactly on the hour appointed!*" He turned.

"Take over, Slim."

"Right, Captain." The gaunt lieutenant whipped a notebook from his pocket. "Gentleman Dan? Check the Meteorological Bureau and find out if there are any falling stars or active comets in the vicinity of these places"—he passed a slip of paper to the man—"and on these dates."

"Pat!" A stocky, red-faced man with a wispy mustache and large feet came over. "Check the fingerprints of those stiffs—Doc will give 'em to you—and see if you can get anything. Also, have a look in the Rogues' Gallery for this mug." He handed him a silhouetted photo. "The man is dead; but we'd still like to know who he is, his connections."

He swung. "Hank?" A big-handed, raw-boned man climbed to his feet. He was a former railroad hand and the latest member of the crew. "Check your shipping contacts and find what, if any, shipments of helium gas are going out of the country. Check any shipments that may have gone out, any shipments of military value, and find if they have been re-shipped from their original destinations."

"Right, Slim." The big man paused. "It'll take a lot of money, if you want speed. I'll have to use long distance 'phones, radios, telegrams—maybe grease a few palms here and there."

Satan cut in. "What do you call speed? How long will this take you?"

"A month."

"A month?" Satan laughed grimly. "The country may be blown

sky-high in a month! The Emperor of the Dead might burn a thousand homes, ten thousand people, in a month." He frowned. "Make it two days," he decided.

"Phew!" Hank breathed. "But—the cost?"

Satan took the envelope from Slim, the envelope with the

Satan's tommy-gun
bit vengefully at the
dark, moving mass.

twenty-thousand dollars found on the dead gunner, tossed it to the man. "Use this as a starter!"

"Yes, Cap'n."

Slim said, "Solly? I'm giving you two addresses—one in New

63

York State, the other in Massachusetts. Get there *fast*. Question the survivors of the fires at those addresses, if you can find any. Servants, maybe. Ask any questions you think would be important in finding out *how* those fires started. And this is essential—ask exactly the same questions at each place."

Then Slim got the attention of them all. "Report to the newly assigned meeting place tomorrow night, whether the work is through or not. We may have further orders. Those who aren't through their work can finish it the day after tomorrow."

He looked down at his list. "Kayo drives the Captain, as usual. Soapy goes along as a bodyguard. I guess that fixes everything."

"Except the dough," Solly piped up. "What do we do, charge it?"

Slim pulled out his bankroll again. "I nearly got away with that one," he grinned. "One thousand dollars each ought to see you through any emergency until tomorrow."

"Slim! The pictures!" Satan said.

"Coming to that, Captain. Men—here are photographs of a certain chap who is now dead. Ask about him wherever you go. See if anybody knows him, what his connections are." His voice sobered.

"But have your hand near your gun when you do ask!"

When the rest of them had left, Satan turned to The Dutchman. "What about that thing? What is it?"

The big fellow turned the cylinder over in his hands. "An air-tight composition that's non-melting, unless under terrific heat." He jiggled it. "I imagine there's some sort of gas in it."

Satan looked meaningly at Slim. He turned to his crew man again. "How can you find out what gas it is? Without burning this shed up?"

The Dutchman's eyebrows came up. "Why do you say that, Cap'n?"

Satan considered. "Suppose I told you a bullet hit a similar cylinder, burst it—and a terrific fire started up, a fire that consumed everything in the vicinity?"

"What color smoke?"

"Black."

The Dutchman handled the cylinder with more respect. "I'd say it was hydrogen gas."

"Ha!" Satan whipped around to Slim. "See the tie-up? Helium—and hydrogen. The two balloon gases. One inflammable, the other non-inflammable."

"Beg your pardon, Cap'n," The Dutchman cut in. "Helium *will* burn—in the raw state—in a mixture of other gases. But it's got to be pretty hot."

"Can you test it safely? Or should we burn it?"

The Dutchman said, "There's no reason why we have to burn it. I'll tell you soon enough." Satan watched the man while he pricked the thing with a pin... but he was to wish later that they had burned it, instead.

A sweetish, sickly-smelling gas hissed out of the cylinder. The Dutchman sniffed, took a bit of candle from his pocket, rubbed it gently over the pin-prick and closed the hole.

"Hydrogen," he said.

Satan nodded. Slim gave the man orders to stand by; but he

thought of something else. "Captain? How about the—*signature?*"

Satan nodded again. "Good man, Slim. The Dutchman can check that, too. Give him the paper. We'll see him tomorrow night and get his report."

**WHEN THE** crew assembled the following night, Satan stood silent while Slim got the reports.

Pat said, "No prints of that gang, Slim. No Rogues' Gallery photos, either."

"Okay. Gentleman Dan?"

"No comets, and the guy asked me what brand of likker I'd been drinking. He said he wanted to steer clear of it, if it made me see comets in two different places on the same night."

The crew members laughed. "Solly?"

The hawk-nosed little man handed over a sheaf of papers. "The whole thing is there, includin' who had babies that day in the neighborhood." Slim took the questions and answers and passed them to Satan.

"Hank?"

"Didn't take any time at all, Slim. I have railroad contacts and shipping contacts near the three helium centers. They said that only enough stuff for use in pinkish signs, in divers suits, and for hospitals had gone out. Three thousand cubic feet would cover the whole thing."

"What does that mean?" Slim asked, puzzled.

"The Macon packed about two and a half *million* cubic feet of helium, Slim," Satan explained. "Three thousand feet isn't worth talking about."

"Dutchman?" Slim continued.

The big chap shook his head slowly. "I don't know," he admitted. "That black stuff, that looks like paper, is a sort of super-asbestos. It's great stuff. I couldn't even light it with a blow-torch. But the coloring on that salamander and the signature—"

Satan was interested. "What's your guess?"

"I'd say it was a sort of enamel, Cap'n, that was baked into the stuff by a terrific heat. If I knew how to make that, I'd be a millionaire."

Satan frowned beneath his mask. "Baked in, eh?" He considered, shook his head. "Can't figure that one out at all." Slim cocked his head at Soapy. Kayo was on guard. "And what did you find out, Soapy?"

The little man started. "Me? I shadowed Cap'n and read the papers—and say!" he ducked into his pocket, "here's a funny one. Remember the creamy container that I threw you?"

"What about it?" Slim asked.

"I can get a grand for it," the little man said, passing Slim an ad he had cut from the paper. Slim stared, started, passed it to Satan.

"Look at this!"

It read, *"One thousand dollars reward for a cream-white transparent cylinder lost on South Street. No questions asked."* It gave a nearby address.

Satan smiled grimly. "Slim, you and I will cover this. The rest of you are to stand by!" They left immediately.

At the address, a slatternly woman admitted them, shook

her head when they showed her the ad. "That party moved today," she said.

"Where was his room? What did he look like?"

"He was a foreigner o' some kind. Japanese, I guess. His room was on the second floor, front."

Satan and Slim bounded up the stairs, despite the woman's protests. They crashed the door, went in with drawn guns. Slim flashed his light, but the place was deserted. They were leaving when the leader saw a coat on a hook in back of the door.

"No harm checking the pockets," he said. He took the garment, shoved his hand into one pocket after another. He stopped, suddenly, came out with a bit of crumpled paper. He spread it out, read:

*We smash Thatcher—Colorado—plant, on the night of the fifteenth.*

"Good Lord!" He shoved the note to Slim. "The fifteenth! That's only two nights from to-night!"

They raced down the stairs and out, were back at the rendezvous in record time.

"Everybody out," Satan snapped. "We're off for Colorado to-night. Guns, ammunition, the usual fighting equipment!" He thought for a moment. "Pack your gas masks, too."

He stopped, calculated rapidly. "We split here, get out there individually, every man for himself. Naturally, we can't travel the highways and airways of the country in masks… so each of you be careful to guard your identities from the other. Satan's Crew is a secret organization, secret even within its ranks!" He looked at them, then said, "Remember! Thatcher, Colorado, by the day after tomorrow. We meet at night, near the gas refining plant. We will be masked!"

Slim stirred. "Just where, at the plant, Captain? It's probably a pretty big place."

"Right! Find the main gate to the plant, pace off exactly five hundred steps, to the east. Look for the most secluded hiding place available and call out your emergency letters. If it's the right spot, you will get an answer... your crew name! Slim and I shall be there first."

# CHAPTER 8
## DEAD-END STREET

IT WAS a windy, starless night. Slate-gray clouds scudded low overhead and the tree-tops rustled nervously. An inky blot in a mass of huge boulders moved, split into two parts.

Silhouetted against the gray clouds stood a disordered squad of dark, barnlike buildings. Crouched low behind a rock in that mass of boulders, one of those twin black dots moved... came erect; tall, gaunt, alert.

"I think someone is coming, Captain!"

Satan melted back in the cup hollowed out by the rocks. A ray of light sprang up suddenly nearby and fingered about the boulders. It snapped off as suddenly.

For minutes that seemed hours, there was no sound other than the rustle of leaves and the soughing of the wind in the branches. Then there was a low, penetrating whistle followed by "G-D. G-D."

Slim cursed flatly. "Gentleman Dan!" he answered huskily in quick response.

One of the rocks sprouted a thin finger of light, a finger that poised for only a second, then blinked out.

"G-D is right," Slim growled. "What was the idea of flashing that light?"

The tall newcomer laughed slightly. "Now, Slim! I've been brought up better than that. I wouldn't do that sort of thing."

"It wasn't you, then?"

"Of course not." Gentleman Dan turned, peered at the back of the hollow. "Evening, Cap'n," he said calmly.

Slim asked, "Who was it?"

"Damned if I know. I've been here two hours now. The place is *alive* with sounds! I didn't dare call my signal letters until those others had gone away."

"What others?"

"I guess you couldn't see so well from down here. There was a small mob hiding out over near that shed, yonder. I could see them moving along the white side of it. One of the men finally broke off, came this way with the light. When he turned back, the others all moved off."

"Where to?" Satan asked swiftly.

"Through the fields there, paralleling the road."

A hissed "S-Y... S-Y," interrupted them.

"Okay, Soapy," Slim said quietly. There was a scraping sound as the next crew man came down into the hollow. Other call letters followed rapidly. "...P-T!"

"Okay, Pat."

## A GHOST RIDES THE DAWN

"H-K!"

"Right, Hank."

"K-O!"

"Right here, Kayo!"

The entire crew was in the hidden cup in a matter of minutes. Slim reached down, brought up a roll of dark material. "Gentleman Dan, you stand guard outside. We'll spread this black canvas and get our orders from the captain. You'll stick close with us, in case we have to split the crew, so you won't need any immediate instructions."

"Right, Slim."

The lanky, nonchalant member of the crew eased away. Slim snapped open some thin, steel rods, quickly fixed them in position, then spread the black canvas head-high in the hollow. The crew members filed silently under the thing. The sides were folded down.

A Satan-lamp jumped alive and lit up the masked faces that were there. Slim's morose eyes passed over them…

…The Dutchman… Pat… Solly… Hank… Kayo… Doc… Soapy. And Gentleman Dan, outside….

"All present, Captain."

"I'll take over, Slim." Satan's face was grim, forbidding, as he circled the masked crew with his eyes. "Gentleman Dan saw a mob near that shed, down the road. Any of you others see anything?"

The masked men nodded. Hank spoke up. "I didn't see anyone near the shed, Cap'n. But someone challenged me from a barn while I was crossing over a field."

"Where?"

"About a half-mile across the road, away from the buildings."

"What was the challenge?"

"I couldn't make it out, Cap'n. The language, I mean. It was *queer*, sort of. As though the man was talking high, and yet through his nose."

"Japanese!" Slim whispered.

Satan nodded. "What did you do, Hank?"

"I ran like hell," the man said. "Back where I'd come from. I doubled over from another direction."

"Lamp, Slim," Satan said tersely. He took the beam in his hand, trained it on the bodies of the men. They were garbed in thin, dull, full-length black capes that buttoned high over the neck. Their feet were shod in thin-skinned shoes with thick, felt soles.

Black gloves blended their hands with the dark, and low, snap-brim black hats were jammed tight on their heads. Satan snapped, "Inspection!"

The gloved hands moved and the capes rippled. Tommy-guns, slung on big hip holsters, came into view. Gas masks were hooked firmly to belts. A coil of rope was wrapped around each man's waist. A bowie knife, sheathed, was also on each belt. The individual armories were completed by a brace of automatics on each man.

"Attention!"

The capes, which permitted full coverage when the man was still, yet offered instant access to the wanted weapon at the slightest movement, fell back into place.

"Orders!"

SLIM STEPPED forward, his elbow touching the leader's. His eyes roved that circle of masks alertly as Satan spoke.

"We're going on to the buildings," Satan said slowly. "What we'll find there, other than the watchmen on duty, I don't know. There are two buildings which are more important than the others. Listen, all of you, and get an idea of what to expect in case of an attack on the plant.

"We can't do anything to stop a mob from destroying the pipes from the gas wells. But no mob can accomplish anything by doing that. The gas is there, under ground, and it would simply mean that a new pipe would have to be driven. So we'll forget the wells. But there are other things. The first step of the method used to separate helium from the other gases, is the washing of the gas to get rid of the carbon dioxide—this is the first and the simplest process.

"After that, the various other gases are let off by *freezing the gas*. Helium has the lowest freezing point… is the last gas to turn liquid. Understand? So, the gas must go through freezing units, and as it hits different stages, different gases are piped off in fluid form."

Solly smiled. "It's de opposite to makin' water from ice, huh? Wit' ice, you *heat* it to make it into water; an' wit' gas, you *freeze* it to make it into water."

Satan nodded. "Thanks, Solly. That's it. So the important buildings in this set up are the freezing units, the compressors that drive the gases through the freezers… and the storage tanks of helium ready for use. If the tanks are smashed, it will cost a fortune to rebuild them; if the helium ready for use is stolen or allowed to escape, it'll be damned expensive."

The men nodded their understanding. "Okay," Satan said, his face eased. "We break into three groups: one bunch for the storage tanks… one for the freezing-unit buildings… and one for the expansion unit, where the pure helium is developed. Assign the men, Slim!"

Satan's lieutenant had already made up his mind. "Hank—Solly—Doc—to watch the storage tanks. Group two—Pat—Soapy—The Dutchman."

Satan cut in. "Group Two—the expansion-unit building. Slim has miniature maps of all the buildings, marking the escapes we can use if we need them. Who does that leave for the freezing-unit building?"

"Yourself—Kayo—Gentleman Dan, and me," Slim told him.

Satan nodded. "Good. Now, in case of an emergency, I'll flash my Satan-lamp on a building that all can see. At a sign like that, you are to cut and run for it. Back to New York. And wait for orders."

Big Hank asked, "Why should we cut and run for it?"

"The Navy Department may be in on this, Hank. I'm not fighting the Navy. Nor do I wish to be killed by the Navy. If any of our own breed opens fire, we're through with it—this part of it, anyway."

Kayo said, "I got our special plane parked under cover, ten miles down the road, Cap'n. The car I brought is down the line a way."

"Good lad, Kayo. Remember that, all of you. If you can't

make your way out of any trouble we may find, run east on the road. We'll meet there, in case of emergency!"

He paused, his eyes holding the men.

"This is a queer business we're up against, fellows. *Very* queer. There are a score of angles to it, but this helium plot angle is the first definite thing we've hit on. What's behind it all, I can't say. *But I'll know by the time this night is over!*

"Handle yourselves carefully! Try to know *who* is attacking, if an attack develops. But remember the location of the car and the plane. I don't want to run you down any dead-end streets!"

## CHAPTER 9
## TRIPLE TRAP

KAYO'S TEETH chattered in the cold of the dark place. Slim nudged him. "Put your hand in your mouth!" he whispered. "That will—" He stopped, tense. Satan's hand was on his arm.

"Hear that noise?" the crew leader asked in a low voice.

A faint creak came clearly to them all… then a *click*.

"We're not the only gang that knows how to use a pass key," Gentleman Dan husked. They fell silent again.

The sound of muffled steps came near, drifted away. Four shadows passed in front of a window opposite, dropped out of sight behind one of the great freezers. They didn't reappear. Satan crouched tense for a moment, then pulled Slim close, spoke into his ear.

*"At the slightest noise, we jump them!"* he said. *"Any noise will mean they are getting the job under way immediately!"*

"What if they're setting a bomb?" Slim asked.

"Then they'll try to get out. It's a cinch they won't do any bombing while *they're* still in here!" Satan said.

Ten minutes more passed… minutes in which the freezing cold of the room ate into the bones of the men. The freezing machines that dropped the gases to a temperature of *minus* 250 degrees, Fahrenheit, had chilled the building with the unendurable cold of an icy Arctic grave.

Satan came up from his crouch, suddenly. A rattling sound came to the men around him. The other three stood, followed their leader as he crept around the side of the machine that screened them from that other group. Suddenly they halted their careful steps again.

Satan was listening intently. He pushed Slim back. "My God!" he said, low. "Someone *else* is coming in the door! Get back!"

The slight creak of the door opening and closing again sounded in the cold stillness. Satan watched, his eyes straining for a glimpse of the newcomers. "It might be someone this other crowd is waiting for," he whispered.

But in another moment they knew that wasn't the answer. Light steps sounded… steps which led to the hiding place of Satan and his men. They stood flat against the machine, holding their breath. Five shadows came into view, paused, started forward again.

Satan, his back pressed hard against a wall of cold metal,

strained back still farther. One of the newcomers had drifted closer than the others, was standing inches from the crew leader. The wraith turned, started to move back to the others, lost his balance for a moment and put his hand out to steady himself—and put his hand squarely on Satan's chest!

The leader acted swiftly, silently. He jammed his hand up, found the man's mouth, closed his palm over it hard. He heaved, lifted the struggling man's feet clear of the ground, where he could make no sound in his frantic efforts to twist loose from that iron grip.

The others of the crew stood over in front of Satan, to screen him from view. But the newly arrived group moved nearer, whispering. One of the strange mob hissed into the darkness. Hissed again. Satan knew why. They were calling the man who had wandered away!

The lightness and small stature of his captive told Satan much that he wanted to know.

…A flat, broad face, wide lips, wide nostrils. "An Oriental," Satan knew. "Probably a Japanese!"

He tried to ease back around the corner of that machine, where he could knock the man senseless with a blow that couldn't be heard by those others. He was succeeding….

But a shot crashed, outside the building; and another followed swiftly. The group standing close to Satan's men jumped. A louder hiss came… then an impatient beam of light sought the man who had strayed away, who was now in Satan's grasp.

There was a gasp from the man training that beam, as the light fell on Satan's masked quartet. Slim jammed his tommy-gun into the glare of it.

"Just hold still," he said in a low voice. "One move—one sound, even!—and I'll hose you!"

Satan heard a shuffling noise over by the window, where the third group lay in hiding. He decided on a desperate move, swung his free arm, crashed a hard fist to his captive's jaw. The man's weight sagged. Satan eased him to the floor, snapped the beam of his Satan-lamp on that other crowd in front of them—prepared to see the replicas of those yellow-faced corpses they had dropped from the wharf.

He gasped. A cluster of frightened little brown men stood in the glare of his lamp. And at their head was Ishii Kokamori, the Japanese naval spy!

The situation was under control—until one of Kokamori's men lost his nerve. With a strangled sob, the man went for his gun and snapped a shot at Satan. Kayo grunted and pulled his trigger.

A crashing roar sounded through the still place. The Jap staggered, stumbled, went down. Another Jap decided to risk his safety on a gun. Satan fired from the hip, his slug tearing the Jap's gun from his hand. The crew leader snapped, "Out into the open, men! This other crowd is closing in!"

Kokamori, who had been standing rigidly quiet, started. The sound of running feet came from across the room. The little brown man twisted his head—and his eyes fell on the satanic figure that loomed over him, that stood threateningly in the circle of light that came from that strong lamp.

And then came the shout from the other side of the room.

"It's Satan! Close in on him, men! Take him at all costs!"

Satan cursed flatly and jammed his revolver in front of him, forcing Kokamori back. "Out! Back up! There's a third mob here someplace. Get going!"

His plan was to clear the building, to take Kokamori with him for safety and for questioning. But the mob from across the room ganged over to the door, flashed a third beam of light on. And a heavy voice reared:

"The F.B.I., Satan! Stand where you are, or by God, we'll blow the daylights out of you!"

Satan gasped. He snapped, "Back out of this, fellows! It's the Feds!"

He jumped around the corner of the machine, his men on his heels. But the crashing roar of gun fire sounded again, and a voice, an American voice, cried, "He's got me! That little brown devil near the other freezer, Jo! *Look out for him!*"

A machine gun stuttered suddenly, then a crashing return volley came. A man screamed horribly. Satan was at a window, smashing at it with his tommy-gun. He knocked the shattered glass from the frame, climbed the sill, vaulted to the ground outside. A patter of feet sounded from nearby. Satan ducked as a blaze of orange flame licked out of the night. A slug slammed into the side of the building.

Gentleman Dan swung down beside him, was raising his tommy-gun. Satan put out a hand, stopped him. "Cut it! That may be a Fed!"

Kayo and Slim came out of the window, then a small man hurled himself over their heads and landed rolling, out in the clear. He came to his feet, chattered a command in Oriental language. A voice answered—and then a dozen slugs ripped the ground near Satan's men.

"Let 'em have it," Satan said grimly.

GENTLEMAN DAN'S tommy-gun snapped alive with the first word. He sprayed the darkness where those shots had come from, crouched and ran along the wall, holding the trigger hard.

Two more men jumped down from the window—G-men.

Satan barked a command to his crew; he raced along the wall and rounded the building. He saw a stand of tank cars near by, jumped for the cover of them. But a high pitched monotone sang out at him and a shot clipped his right ear.

Satan poured a burst of fire into the mouth of that other

flame, and a man went down, gasping. A fusillade opened up behind. The G-men were on the trail, their guns blazing. Gentleman Dan cursed suddenly, stumbled, went down. But he was up in a flash.

The crew pounded around a tank car, and a man stepped out into the half light, a tommy-gun in his hands. Slim yelped, "S-M" just as he levelled his own gun.

"D-C," came the calm answer.

"Gang in here, Doc," Satan snapped. "We're drifting. The Feds are in this!"

"Hank! Solly!" Slim shouted. Two shadows loomed around the end of the car, but a volley of fire burst from directly underneath the big tank-trucks. Hank gasped and went down. Satan stopped, jammed his gun low, fired a long burst.

Feet were pounding along the other side of the car, but Satan's lamp sprang alive, streaked over Hank's features. The man was dead, the side of his face ripped away. And at that moment a shadow tore around the end of the car, a gun coming up in its hand.

Kayo calmly swung his automatic and *thucked* the attacker sharply. It was a G-man. He went down like a sledged steer. The crew darted across to another car, rounded it, came near another building. Satan snapped the switch of his lamp, trained the lens on the wall.

The giant figure of Satan sprang into clear view—the signal for the retreat!

There was a call from nearby. The Dutchman yelled out his letters, and Pat and Soapy right after him. But a squad of little men appeared, almost under their feet, and snapped a half-dozen shots into the crew.

Slim cursed with pain. Satan and Doc hammered a terrific volley into the new attackers, and the men melted from in front of them. The crew raced on between two buildings, dug for the road. At a challenge, they stopped. Two men ahead had stepped from behind a tree. Satan grunted.

"Damn it. They're Feds. We can't open up on 'em."

Slim snarled, "Charge them! Maybe they'll get a couple of us; but we're bound to get by, a few of us."

The problem was settled for them when a trio of men scudded low from the other side of the building and tried to clear past the two G-men. But the Feds saw them, ripped a burst of fire into them. One of the trio fell, but the other two whirled, blasted at the Federal agents. The gun fight lasted about thirty seconds, and when it was over, the trio had melted to the earth, the G-men were sprawled flat.

A fresh burst of firing came from far behind them, moving in another direction. Satan listened. "The Federals and the rest of that other gang are shooting it out. Thank God they're in another direction!"

He started to run again… but suddenly he paused. He snapped his lamp on, moved close to the fallen Feds. One of the men moved, batted his eyes, smiled faintly. "Finish it," he whispered. "Finish it… *Satan!*"

The crew leader blinked, stared at the man. He lay on his back, blood running down over his face. Satan shuddered. "I'm not fighting you men," he said quietly. He listened to the receding fire from the other side of the plant, stepped quickly to the trio who had tried to pass the Federal agents and had failed in the attempt.

His lamp traced them out. He whistled. "Slim! Here's Kokamori."

The Japanese spy's eyes were glittering brightly in the light of the lamp. "Voice—I know," he gasped. "Voice—I have heard before!"

Satan shook his head. "I'm not answering that, Kokamori. But maybe you'll answer me, before I'm through."

The man shook a denial. "Kokamori—not wish to speak to—Emperor of the Dead! Emperor of the Dead—enemy to my country—" The man gasped painfully—"enemy to own country—*too*. Kokamori not speak!"

Satan started. "What? You think I'm the Emperor of the Dead?"

The Japanese agent smiled fixedly, nodded his head. He didn't speak.

Satan turned. "Kayo! Dutchman! Gentleman Dan! I don't want to leave this fellow and that wounded G-man lying here. Get them up on your backs. It'll be a tough load, I know—but we've got to do what we can for them, right away."

Gentleman Dan limped up. Satan took one look at him and motioned him away. "I didn't know they'd nicked you, Dan. Here, I'll take Kokamori myself."

He swung the little Jap up in his arms and the grim line of men started the long trek to the hidden automobile.

Satan's crew had paid dearly. Gentleman Dan had been shot through the leg; and Slim had a flesh wound in his shoulder.

...While Big Hank, the solemn, quiet, serious ex-railroad man, lay in that gory yard they had left, his dead face turned up to the starless sky.

# CHAPTER 10
# A FLASH IN THE NIGHT

THE BATTERED band gathered in a clearing in the dense woods. Snuggled close to the tree line, in a large flat field, loomed the speedy cabin plane that Kayo had piloted to the scene.

Two shielded Satan-lamps cast a faint light on the group squatted in a circle.

Satan sat on the running board of the car in which they had traveled from the fight scene. The cushions and seats had been stripped from the car for the badly wounded G-man and the Japanese spy. Doc, the medical member of the crew, was squatting beside Kokamori, his eyes on the man and an inquiring finger on his pulse.

A few feet beyond, the wounded Federal man had been made comfortable on some cushions and coats. Both his arms had been broken, and his scalp furrowed by Japanese bullets. But every now and again he opened his eyes to stare at Satan.

Doc stood up, shaking his head slightly.

"How is he?" Satan asked.

Kokamori, his black eyes overly bright and his face yellowish in the light, smiled weakly. "Ishii Kokamori—going to die," he said slowly. "Ishii Kokamori shot many times, through belly. He go to ancestors." He paused, his face sad and disappointed.

"Kokamori verree sorry he not kill you—*Emperor of the Dead!*"

Satan stared, thunderstruck. "What?" Then he laughed, a note of bitterness in his voice. "Why, you rat—one of my men was killed tonight, and two others wounded! And all because of your work! I would have sworn that you weren't in with the Emperor… as he styles himself. But now I've changed my mind!"

Kokamori blinked. He started to believe Satan, then doubted him with a slight smile. But at Satan's expression, he sobered again. "You not Emperor of the Dead?"

The Federal man's eyes were hard. "I know damn well who you are," he said flatly. "You're Satan—Captain Satan! Man, I'd give ten years of my life to get my hands on you!"

"Wait till you're out of those splints first," Satan said. He turned his eyes to the Jap. "Well? The F.B.I. has given you the dope, Kokamori." He laughed softly. "Why don't you drop the act and admit who you are—that *you're* working for the Emperor of the Dead?"

But the Jap was trying to rise, struggling feebly. Doc put a restraining hand on him. "Easy there, man. You're going fast enough. Don't aggravate that hemorrhage!"

"F.B.I.," the little man panted. "F.B.I., you say? Is that a joke, pliss?"

"Listen," the G-man said through his teeth. "Things are bad enough without your trying to kid me. What the hell *did* you think I was?"

But Kokamori wasn't listening, had swung to stare at Satan again. "You—you not Emperor of the Dead! And this man—this man, he F.B.I. Then why do men of Emperor of the Dead trap and capture me—speak of making raid on Thatcher plant?"

Satan was on his feet. He jumped near Kokamori and crouched low. "Listen, Kokamori—is that true?"

The Jap nodded. "They catch me, lock me in room. I hear talk, and they say they raid plant for helium and to destroy the tanks. I escape, burning chair ropes with candle—and come here to block Emperor."

The F.B.I. man was in it now. "What? Why, Jo Desher was trapped by some Japs—navy agents, he said—and he heard *them* making plans to raid Thatcher. He escaped, too, and—" The G-man paused, his eyes wide and on Satan. The crew leader was standing again, a great light of intelligence dawning on him.

"It fits," he said quietly. Briefly, he told the story of the advertisement, of his answering it and finding the 'clue-note' in a discarded coat. Kokamori's face was tragic for a moment; then he sighed, smiled again.

"You Captain Satan, pliss? Very sure? You great Satan who fight criminal men—and make F.B.I. mad, too?"

"I'm Satan," the leader answered. He picked up a lamp, thrust it close to the side of the automobile. The Satanic mark stood forth boldly in the circle of light. "There's my brand!"

"Ah," the little man sighed. "Emperor of the Dead very clever man! *Verre* clever. Emperor know that I—Kokamori—am after him. He know you—Satan— are after him. He know F.B.I. are after him, too."

The G-man cursed quietly. "So he pitted us against one another, eh?" He thought for a moment. "But if you were after the Emperor of the Dead, both of you—why did you spray the F.B.I.?"

"I not know who attack," Kokamori said. "Man shoot gun outside in yard—I flash on light, see Satan. Fight starts. I do not know who it can be except Emperor of the Dead!" He paused, laughed weakly.

"Emperer of the Dead make sucker of us all!" he said, slangily.

SATAN STARED his doubt. "I'm not sure you're telling the full truth, Kokamori. For instance—*why* were you fooling around Thatcher at all? What business is it of yours what the Emperor of the Dead does in the United States?"

"Answer very easy," Kokamori said. "Emperor of the Dead, he promise huge supply of helium to—" he hesitated—"enemy country to mine. He want, in return, great power when enemy bomb Japan from high up, in super-bombing ship. Kokamori work to keep helium from him."

"Nuts!" the agent said. "Then why track Desher?"

"Easy, too, that answer! Desher, he look for Emperor. I, Kokamori, cannot find Emperor. Maybe Desher find. I follow Desher."

Satan considered a moment. "Kokamori? Did it strike you that it was too *easy*, the way you escaped?"

The Jap's lips were compressed in a sudden spasm of pain.

But he nodded. After a minute he spoke; but very faintly. "All very clear now. I escape easy, Desher escape easy too, maybe; and Satan, he find note in pocket."

"It was a triple trap, all right," Satan admitted. "And now we're right back where we started. But on this I'll take an oath—that neither I nor any of my crew fired a shot at the F.B.I. The only men we cracked down on were Kokamori's bunch."

"Maybe," the F.B.I. man said. But his eyes were convinced.

Satan snapped his fingers suddenly, then stooped to unlace Kokamori's shoes. He stripped them off, felt the soles of his feet. Then he stood up again.

"Why you do that, pliss?"

"I just wanted to see if you were a—*fire cultist!* If you were, your feet would be hard as bricks!"

Kokamori smiled, gently at first, then more and more widely. His eyes were mere slits.

"You very smart man, Satan! Kokamori think that he alone knows this. But Kokamori is happy, now. His soul go to ancestors gladly. Kokamori think Captain Satan maybe catch Emperor of the Dead."

"How do you know about that foot business?" Satan asked. But he got no answer. He stepped nearer, impatiently. "Answer me, Kokamori!"

Doc interrupted, speaking softly. "Ishii Kokamori is answering questions far more important than yours, Cap'n. Ishii Kokamori is giving an account of the stewardship of his soul… to his ancestors!"

The group was silent for a moment, then the Federal man stared at Satan. "What the hell is this 'fire-cultist' talk?"

Satan looked back at him steadily. "What do you make of the case?"

"None of your damn business!"

"Then don't ask me any questions." But he tensed suddenly, his head cocked. A roaring sound was coming from far away, growing with each second. The Federal man took a slow, deep breath, but Satan saw him. He motioned to Slim. "Automobiles coming!"

The tall lieutenant of the crew gently but firmly shoved a gag into the agent's mouth. The man's eyes were raging, but he was helpless. The sound came nearer, a flick of lights showed in the sky some distance away. Two automobiles hammered by, about a half a mile away. Then the sounds died into the night.

"There go your pals," Satan said. Slim removed the man's gag.

"They'll be back!"

Satan shook his head. "I don't think so." He grinned. "But I'm not gambling on it any. I'm leaving guards posted where they can do me the most good. If they stopped near here, we'd be away in the plane in thirty seconds." He turned to Slim. "Come over here a minute, Slim."

THE GAUNT man followed Satan to a point some distance from the Federal man. "This thing is getting screwier every minute. You hear what I said to Kokamori about the fire-cultists?"

Slim nodded. "You still had Kokamori lined up with that

gang who jumped us at the wharf. But suppose the men are—er—what did you say?"

"Slim! Fire-cultists worship fire, use it as a cleansing power. I've seen some of their secret rituals, in Japan and China. They will do anything—up to and including murder!—to *cleanse* a person, as they call it. That's the weird thing about this set-up. That—and the comets."

Slim shook his head. "All right, Captain. So they're fire-cultists. So what? Why does that one fact make you think there's something screwy about their connection with the Emperor of the Dead?"

"Just this," Satan told him. "These cultists will go to any lengths, as far as their religion is concerned. But they will have absolutely nothing to do with crime—ordinary crime. The business of extortion, and the connivance of the cult with some warring government—is the one false note in the entire set-up! That—and the comets, as I said before."

Slim scratched his head. "I'm beginning to see what you mean."

"This Emperor of the Dead," Satan continued, "has somehow brought the cult under his power. Don't ask me how. But all he's after is *money*. He's using the cult to *cleanse* people—unless these people kick in money to him. Do you get it?"

Slim nodded. "But why do you say the comets are false? What have they to do with it?"

"Nothing. In some way this devil—whoever he is, and wherever he is—has the ability to produce the *illusion* of a comet.

Maybe he has a balloon of some sort, that he releases at the time of a fire. Or a rocket!"

Both men were silent, and Satan paced the small clearing.

"I'm stumped," he muttered after a moment. "Led into a trap, like a sheep to the slaughter, one of my men killed—and up against a stone wall!"

He paused, listening intently. "Slim! Don't you hear the sound of a motor?"

The lieutenant listened a moment. Then he walked a few steps through the clearing, stopped again. "There it is! I can—" A faint throbbing had come on the night air, then died down again. "It's gone, now."

After five minutes, it hadn't come to them again. Satan sat down on the running board with Slim at his side. He fished Solly's report from his pocket, studied with keen eyes the answers to half a hundred questions.

He snapped his fingers suddenly. "Slim! Here's a point we might check on, in these reports! Service men from gas companies were at *both* houses, on the day of the fires!" His brows contracted. *"Gas companies."*

Slim stood up, his eyes hard. "I'll get Solly and raise hell. He didn't go to see those inspectors."

Satan's eyes were shining with excitement. "It wouldn't have done any good, Slim! It wouldn't have meant a thing. For the very simple reason that there *were* no gas inspectors. This is one coincidence too many. Why—in two widely separated places—should *gas inspectors* appear just before a fire?"

"You think they had something to do with it?"

91

"I know they had! Look, Slim—helium gas… hydrogen gas… and gas inspectors! There's some queer hookup there."

Slim was thoughtful. He stared up at the heavens through the trees, turning the thing over in his mind. He blinked, passed a hand across his face, blinked again. He came to his feet slowly, head back, eyes up.

"Captain! What's that fiery thing up there, that blaze I can see in the sky?"

Satan swung, his eyes puzzled. The Federal man, some distance away, called: "How about that, Satan? *Now* do you believe in comets?"

The crew leader's face was taut.

In the sky, far above—farther by miles than any plane could climb, even any stratosphere balloon—a blaze was cutting a path across the heavens.

"The comet!" Satan marvelled.

He watched as the flaming body streaked across the sky at incredible speed. Suddenly it swooped in a downward arc and shot toward the earth. Nearer and nearer it loomed. Satan raised his voice in the hush:

"Dutchman!"

"Yes, Cap'n?"

"What do you make of that. A falling star?"

"No, Cap'n. A star coming on like that, this near the earth, would draw us, by its attraction, into a terrific collision." He pondered. "It isn't a comet, either."

Satan started suddenly, cocked his head. There was a sputtering noise from somewhere above… a sputtering and a swishing rush of air.

"A plane!" The crew leader rasped.

Kayo came on the run. "Where?" he asked his chief.

Satan stared, listened. "I can't see anything," he said. "It's not a plane on normal business, or it would show its running lights." He sighed. "Start our plane, Kayo! I think this is the one break I've been needing!"

"What's your plan?" Slim asked. "Remember the tie-up, Slim? A comet—and a fire? Evidently we have another little bit of fire-extortion in the vicinity someplace. We'll push up and have a look around!"

The sputtering from the air sounded louder. Satan stared up, saw the 'comet' die down, fade entirely. But the sputtering noise came louder, nearer. The prop of Kayo's ship had started up with a roar, then quieted to a warming speed.

"Slim!" Satan snapped. "You're coming with me and Kayo. Have the rest of the men stay here until dawn. If we don't report back, they are to go to New York and wait orders at their usual places. The Federal man can be held for a while, tended by one of the men, and then deposited at some far-off ranch… safely."

Slim ran to assign the men, give out the orders. Satan walked near the Federal agent. "Sorry for your smash-up," he said. "But Doc says it's nothing serious."

"Where you going?" the F.B.I. man asked sourly.

"Comet chasing! This is one coincidence too many! If I have any luck, Desher can sit on his fanny again. I'll—"

A sudden roar sounded nearby. A plane flashed overhead, at

93

about a thousand feet, its motor wide, and made a steep bank. Satan shouted:

"Slim! Come on! There's some hookup between this plane and that 'comet!' If we lose that bird, we may lose our chance to get to the bottom of this thing."

The crew leader and his lieutenant climbed into the cabin of the plane. Kayo riffed the motor once, then slammed his throttle open and roared across the field in a take-off.

The mystery plane had disappeared.

# CHAPTER 11
# THE LINK FAILS

KAYO PULLED the speedy plane up in a steep climb. He banked slightly as he went. Satan and Slim scanned the dark, outside the cabin windows, searching for some sign of the vanished ship.

"That plane must have had some motor trouble," Satan reasoned to his lieutenant. "He was gliding down, fighting the thing—and got it going again just off the ground."

Slim sat hunched in his seat, his eyes alert. "If we only had some idea of his destination, of where he is headed."

"Bend away from Thatcher, Kayo,"

Satan said. "We don't want to start the Federal men up again."

The pilot obediently swung off to the south, continued to fly in a wavering line, staring out and below for any sign of the vanished plane. Satan sat forward suddenly, his eyes keened.

## A GHOST RIDES THE DAWN

"Look! Down below us, Kayo, silhouetted against that sandy patch! See that shadow?"

The pilot whipped the plane in a steep bank, straightened. "Right you are, Cap'n! That's the plane!"

"Lose altitude," Satan ordered. "I don't want that bird to see us. Get close to his level and try to stay within eye-sight of him!"

They flew levelly and cautiously for more than an hour when Kayo cut back and circled again. "I've lost him, Cap'n."

Kayo cut back, circled carefully. Satan ran to the controls, slid into the seat next Kayo. "Give me the stick," he ordered. "You and Slim get your guns ready! I just spotted the plane... trying to make a landing down below."

The ship below was visible to them all, now. It was circling a grove of trees, was dropping lower and lower.

The black of night was now laced with the purplish streaks of dawn. The ship slid through the murk in a driving slip, then Satan ruddered into it and dropped fast for the small field. The other plane was rolling to a stop.

Satan whipsawed the rudder, swinging the crate right and left as he nosed in, and killing the speed. He set the wheels down gently, then rolled rapidly ahead.

The cabin door slammed open behind him and a rattle of gunfire deafened him. He stepped on the brakes as he ranged up near that other plane. Slim and Kayo swarmed down, the tommy-guns in their hands. A man was running across the field.

Kayo and Slim fired a burst over his head, but Satan stopped

them with a shout. He
was running for that
other plane, sprinting
like mad across the
gap of twenty yards
that separated the two
ships.

The plane, its
motor still idling,
stood directly over a
small, cream-colored
cylinder. And near
that cylinder was a
wad of burning paper. Satan left his feet in a dive and stretched
desperately. He landed on his chest and slid the last five feet.

With a final effort, he flipped his hand and knocked the
burning paper aside. Kayo and Slim trotted up, their eyes wide.
Satan rolled out from under the plane, picked up the creamy
cylinder gingerly.

"Must be something pretty important about that ship," he
said grimly. "I imagine that other lad didn't know we were
around at all until we slid in alongside him. Probably thinks
we're ghosts!"

He walked fifty yards away, put the cylinder on the ground,
calmly fired a bullet into it. A flash of flame spouted up, and a
dense cloud of black smoke. The gas burned rapidly, then died
down. "I feel better with that thing out of the way," Satan said.

He was turning back to the mystery plane when something caught his eye.

The cylinder had been consumed by the flames. The fire had died. The smoke had cleared. But in that scorched space where it had burned so brightly was something else.

The black square of paper with a bright red salamander and that signature...

*The Emperor of the Dead!*

SATAN PASSED his hands across his eyes once, blinked, looked again. There was an ironic smile on his face when he walked over and stooped to pick the thing up. It was still hot. He dropped it, watched it flutter back to the ground. Slim and Kayo stood at his side, their eyes wide.

"Where did that thing come from?" Slim asked.

"Inside the cylinder," Satan told them quietly.

"What? Why, how could it be inside the cylinder?"

"Remember what The Dutchman said— 'The coloring is a type of enamel that is baked in by heat'? And, 'The paper is some sort of super-asbestos'?" Both men nodded. Satan shrugged. "What a lot of time I'd have saved if I'd let him burn that cylinder *then,* instead of pricking it."

"How is that, Captain?"

"Don't you see? This asbestos material is white—*when it was packed inside the cylinder!* And so is the enamel coloring matter. The fire of the gas does the cooking, bakes the color in *red...* and turns the paper black."

"Captain, do you feel all right?" Slim asked anxiously.

Satan smiled slightly. "Never better. And never more like

kicking myself! Remember, Slim—the notes were found in the places where the fires had taken place. Right? How did they get there?"

"You tell me," Slim said, doubtfully.

"They were *carried* there! Carried and put there—by The Emperor of the Dead, or one of his *subjects!*—as Kokamori called them."

"But why the comets, Captain?"

"Just to add mystery to a very simple matter. Every time there was a fire, people saw what they took to be a comet. And some folks—in the know—" he smiled slightly, "added that to this other mystery… the mystery of the signature note."

He stood in thought for a moment, then turned and walked back to the strange plane. Slim and Kayo followed him, their eyes puzzled. But they had too much knowledge of Satan's past work to question his judgment… until they could flatly contradict him with evidence.

Now the leader of the crew smiled broadly, pointed to a queer contraption that was slanted up out of the open pit of the plane. He climbed up on the stirrup. "Jump up on that other side, you fellows, and have a look at this!"

Obediently, Slim and Kayo climbed up, stared down at the long metal cylinder that started at the very floor of the plane and cocked up above the pit coaming.

"What do you make of that?" Slim asked.

Satan didn't speak. He was staring at an oblong box that was built onto the cockpit floor. He flipped open the lid… and whistled at the cylindrical objects he saw in the box.

"They look like long sausages with little fans on 'em, don't they?" he asked. He lifted one out, handling it gingerly. Slim's eyes traveled from the affair to the metal 'gun' that grew out of the plane flooring.

"Hell!" he said disgustedly.

Satan looked at him soberly. "That's right, Slim."

Kayo scratched his head. "What's right? What is this thing, anyway?"

"This, as you call it, Kayo, is a sort of aerial torpedo—'comet' to you. I imagine the thing can shoot pretty high… especially when taken to a level of, say, twenty thousand feet, and popped off from there."

Kayo blinked, then pulled the 'gun' open by a ring handle. There was a powerful steel spring in the thing… a spring that was wide-extended, 'sprung,' at the moment. He shoved down, grunted. "It's a powerful baby."

"It's got to be," Satan murmured, "to get this thing away from the pilot's eyes. Gunpowder and hydrogen aren't nice things to have go off in your face. They burn like hell, you know."

He twisted and turned the cylinder in his hand, puzzled. There was a small key on the flat base of it. Satan started to turn it, thought better of it. He opened the 'gun,' put the torpedo into place.

"Let's see if it works," he said.

HE TIGHTENED the spring with a crank, which was evidently there for the purpose. Then he took the cylinder, turned the key, jammed the thing into its case hurriedly. Slim and Kayo started away from the plane; but Satan stopped them.

99

"If the pilot didn't get hurt sitting right over the thing, then we aren't liable to be hurt."

A full minute they waited; then Satan detected a smell of something burning. He reached over and yanked a pin that protruded from the side of the gun casing. The lid of the thing snapped open and there was a sudden rush of air.

The three men blinked, but they turned their heads up a moment later when an explosion sounded high overhead.

In the growing light, the flame was weak; but as the torpedo catapulted higher, into the air, it blazed brighter and brighter. Satan bit his lip. "I nearly slipped that time! I forgot to yank the pin that released the spring—another ten seconds and we'd all have been blown sky-high."

"It didn't do any harm," Slim said. "That was nice figuring, Captain."

Satan turned and stared into the woods, in the direction taken by the pilot of the mystery ship. "I hope it didn't do any harm," he said thoughtfully. "That chap *thought* his scheme to set fire to this crate had succeeded. If he's in the immediate neighborhood now, he knows that it didn't."

Kayo was still staring up into the sky. "What makes her go so high?" he asked. "It's *still* zooming—and I'll bet it's all of twenty-thousand feet up, now!"

"Notice that little fan?" Satan asked. "That's a propeller. The spring fires it into the air… the gunpowder goes off, pushing it faster; the prop turns on what is probably a light, strong spring. Then the heat from the powder reaches the gas and explodes it. That's your fire. Allow a climb of forty or fifty thousand feet for that thing, and twenty for your plane before it shoots it—and that's the illusion of the comet."

Kayo swore his admiration, but Satan was stepping fast again. He snapped open the lid of the little supply compartment of the plane and looked in it. He fished out two of the cream-colored cylinders, slipped one into his pocket under his cape, passed the other one to Slim.

"We'll take these along, just in case," he said. He turned to Kayo. "Jump your plane off, circle away from that town, and dig back to where the boys are. I want them all here—except the one who's to stay with the F.B.I. man."

Satan stooped and set his automatic lighter to the fabric of the plane. When a patch of it was burning, he stepped away.

"We'll drop these masks of ours going into town," he told Slim. "But carry your tommy-gun under your cape, and fold the cape over your arm. I'm going to call New York. If I don't hear what I expect to, then this fork of the trail has petered out, and we'll have to start all over again. But I think we're on our last lap!"

## CHAPTER 12
## THE LONG ROAD TO HELL

S ATAN AND Slim prowled the quiet town, located a small hotel, outside of which was a small sign indicating that there was a telephone inside. Satan led the way. A man snored peacefully in a large easy chair. The lobby—really an old-fashioned parlor—was otherwise deserted.

101

In a corner was a ramshackle 'phone booth. Satan turned to Slim. "You go out and dig up a can of coffee. This alleged hotel isn't awake yet. I'll call New York—" Satan paused to fish out a handful of change, then took the silver coins that Slim gave him—"I'll call New York and check on one important point before we do anything else."

"Right, Captain. But remember, it's two hours earlier in New York!"

"Two hours *later*, Slim!"

The lieutenant grinned. "That's right. I can't keep that straight." He went out the door.

Satan shut the door of the booth and spoke in a low voice to the operator. He had long-distance quickly enough, but he was ten minutes waiting for his New York state connection. He finally had it.

"Hello!... Is this the *Metro Gas Company?*... It is?... How quickly can you tell me if you had a service man at the Marravale home on—" He paused, frowned "What's that? Of course I know it burned down! Now, can you tell me if you had a service man there on that day? Or on the day before?"

He held the wire impatiently. Suddenly, he stood straight in the booth. "You *didn't?*... Are you *sure?*... All right.... Not for *two months* before the fire, eh?" He dropped the receiver on the hook, was ready for his next call.

"...Hello, is this the Hamden Gas Company?... Can you tell me if you had a service man at the Greeson home a short time before the fire?... Yes.... That's right...."

A smile softened his face when he got the same answer. The voice said, "No."

"Solly's report showed two 'gas' inspectors were at the home the day of the fire, in each case," he mused. "Probably flashed their badges—faked badges—and went right on through." But he sobered suddenly.

"How?" he wondered, "did they set those hydrogen bombs off without getting involved themselves, without being burned... or caught, running from the fire?"

He gave it up, was about to push the door of the booth open. But he stopped suddenly, his face hard and his eyes narrowed. The sun was coming in through the windows... and it cast before it the shadow of a man who was standing near the booth... listening!

Satan saw in a flash it wasn't Slim's shadow. He watched that dark silhouette on the floor, saw the squat broadness of it... saw the shadow of the automatic that the man held in his hand. Satan started talking again... as if still carrying on a telephone conversation. But he kept his eyes riveted to that shadow.

Closer and closer, it crept, and the gun-shadow on the floor started up... came higher....

Still talking, Satan eased his tommy-gun out from under his cape. His back hard against the wall, he got the muzzle raised. His fingers fumbled for the trigger, found it just as a wide, yellow face slid into view of the booth window.

Satan jammed down hard.

The terrific roar of the machine gun in the booth smashed at his ear-drums. Glass flew in thousands of splinters, and the

103

door of the booth jigged with the slugs that tore through it. The gunner outside staggered, reeled back into the lobby as the rain of lead smashed him with the force of a hundred hammers.

Satan kicked the wrecked door open, came out with his gun smoking and at ready. But the other man had enough… enough for twenty men. He came up on tiptoe, the gun slipping from his nerveless grasp.

The man who had been sleeping in the easy chair was struggling to get up, his mouth wide and his eyes round with horror. He gaped at Satan, goggled at the gunman, tried to shove himself erect.

But just then the gunner's knees lost their glue… and he toppled on the hotel man, knocking him flat in the chair again. SATAN DARTED out into the street, covering the tommy-gun with the cape over his arm. Slim was running down the street, a coffee can jiggling in his right hand. Satan started walking to the corner rapidly. Slim caught him as he rounded it.

"What was that shooting, Captain? What happened?"

"Man tried to sneak up on me in the booth. But I found what I wanted to, Slim! Those gas inspectors were phonies! Hydrogen bombs did the job."

"But how did they work it? Did they plant the things? After all, if they were gas inspectors and got past the G-men who were stationed there after the extortion notes had been received, they must have put on *some* sort of show!"

"That's what I intend to find out. And when I do, I'll spike the Emperor of the Dead for keeps."

"How?"

"Other extortion notes must be working right now. The thing to do is get that phony gas inspector when he calls at the *next* house to be burned. We can plant men at threatened houses. He's bound to use the same system—the Emperor. It's working now, so why shouldn't it keep working?"

"And what will you do with them? Suppose you spot him on the job?"

"That's simple." They had covered several blocks now, and looking back they saw some citizens hurrying along the street toward the hotel. "I'll trail him if it takes a thousand men to do the job. I'll trail him, and at the end of the road I'll find my man."

Satan stepped around a clump of bushes, stared about him. "We'll have to wait for Kayo to pick us up in the plane. If we can find a spot to lie low in, we'll beat it for the field when we hear the plane coming." He was silent for a moment.

"Why not go there now?" Slim asked.

"Now, Slim!" Satan was gently rebuking. "We know that we're being watched. The fellow spotting me in the 'phone booth was the tip-off to that! If we're not careful, the rest of the crew will be trapped. I don't want to take any chances on having things happen until the boys get here."

"That's right," Slim nodded. "If anything happened to us, the gang would start looking and run right into trouble—capture, maybe."

Satan smiled slightly. "We ought to find something to interest us right here, Slim! It shouldn't be hard to find yellow-faced men with brick-hard feet in a Colorado town!"

"And if we do find one, a yellow man? What'll we do? Trail him to China or Japan, or wherever his headquarters are?"

"Right! To the ends of the earth, if necessary!"

Satan saw a lane that led through a thick stand of trees. Beyond, about two miles away, a barren hill rose. He signaled Slim and made his way across quickly, along the lane and out of sight of the town.

"We can lie low, down this way, until the excitement over the shooting dies down. With the boys on the way here, I can't take any chances of our being stopped and questioned."

They plodded steadily onward, and soon, turning a bend in the wooded path, came suddenly on a group of colorful buildings set close against the rocky hill.

A dark red bungalow was nestled snugly against the hillside. To the right, a black barn made a striking contrast. Cows grazed in the pasture in front of it. They went more slowly, Satan's eyes taking in the place. Opposite the barn, a red and black wellhouse stood several feet away from a grove of shade trees.

"We'll double through that grove, over beyond the well-house. We can see and hear the plane from there, without anyone seeing *us*." But both men stopped suddenly, their heads snapping around in the direction of the bungalow… from which a cheery but feeble voice hailed them.

"Hallo, there! Looking for someone, strangers?"

"That's a bad break," Satan muttered. "We can't duck away

without getting that man suspicious!" He craned his neck, located the speaker.

It was a frail, elderly man, who sat in a chair on the bungalow porch, his head against the high backrest of his chair. "Come over! Come over!" the gray-haired, kindly-faced man invited them.

Satan forced a smile. "Thanks! But we don't want to bother you, sir. We're just—roaming around."

"Won't you come over for a few minutes, then? I don't get a chance to talk with people often, not even the folks in my own town."

"Come on," Satan said to Slim in a low voice. "We can afford to humor him for a few minutes." His eyes drifted to the bulge of the bandage under Slim's jacket, where Doc had dressed that shoulder wound. There was a dark, wet stain on the black material of the jacket.

"You got hurt in an automobile accident," he muttered, as he led the way. "If he asks for names, leave it to me."

They approached the bungalow, Satan's eyes taking in the man's thin, kindly face—the sparkling blue eyes that were set off colorfully by his tanned skin. "It's kind of you," the crew leader said in a low, pleasant voice. "We've had an automobile wreck a few miles from here. We're waiting for friends to pick us up."

"I, too, have been waiting for friends," the man smiled benignly. "But I wait no longer! Come up and have seats, gentlemen." He tapped a gong on the table beside him with a tiny hammer, sending a melodious note through the fresh morning air.

"I am taking the liberty of serving you with coffee." His eyes fell on Slim's coat as the lieutenant followed Satan onto the porch. "Oh! You were injured?"

"Slightly," Slim nodded. His eyes were on the light blanket that lay across the man's lap and stretched to the ground. For the first time, they saw that the old man sat in a wheel-chair.

"I can sympathize with a fellow sufferer," the elderly man smiled. He drew the blanket from the chair and tossed it to one side.

The man's legs had been amputated at the knees.

## CHAPTER 13
## HELL'S HOUSE

A HEAVY-SET, muscular man answered the table gong. Of about medium stature, he had a barrel chest, powerful arms, meaty legs. His round black eyes were set in a stolid mask of a face. His hair was short-cropped, shiny-black.

"You rang, Mr. Phineas!"

It was a hard, flat voice that spoke, and the words were more an accusation than a question. The elderly man nodded his grayed head gently. "Yes, Mark. Coffee for the gentlemen."

He smiled easily when the man disappeared again. "Mark is a rather stolid chap. He hasn't my curiosity about people and places and things." He gestured to the stumps of his legs, stumps that were concealed by the rounded tailoring of the trouser-legs.

"Just being able to get about seems to be enough for him. But if he had been confined to a wheel-chair for twenty years—!" A gentle sigh of resignation escaped him.

He caught himself, smiled apologetically. "But there I go again, rambling oh about *my* misfortunes, and I haven't even introduced myself! My name is Newton D. Phineas, gentleman—cripple—recluse—and in a small measure—philosopher!"

Satan put out his hand. "My name is Emory," he said glibly. "And my friend—" Slim bowed slightly—"is Mr. Gerard."

The crew leader took that slender, graceful hand in his strong, browned one. He blinked, covered his surprise by turning to Slim. "I'm glad we came over this way, Jerry. It was a happy accident."

"Jerry?" the cripple echoed, his hand still in Satan's.

"Nickname," Satan said, releasing that other hand. His eyes went to the hard-tire wheels of the chair. The old gentleman chuckled.

"It's been many a year since anyone called me by *my* nickname," he said. "*Newton* is so severe, so formal."

"What did your friends call you?" Satan asked.

" '*Newt*,' "the man said. "Newt, for short." He smiled genially.

The man Mark appeared with the coffee. He put the steaming cups on the table. Phineas picked up the cup nearest him, drank the steaming-hot stuff with evident relish. Slim put out his left hand and took a cup.

"I like cream with mine," Satan said. He looked at Slim. "I'm afraid you're going to have trouble with that, fellow."

"Eh? Trouble with what?" Phineas was concerned, anxious.

"He's not left-handed," Satan explained. "That bad right shoulder will bother him."

Slim laughed. "I can manage... but I don't want to spill any on the porch." He walked near the rail, raised the cup quickly, then came back to set it on the saucer. It was empty. "Got a few drops on my lapel," he smiled at Satan. "No cream? That's tough on you."

Phineas said, "Dear me, how unfortunate! Mark and I never use cream!"

"That's all right," Satan's voice was hearty. "The milk you get from those cows will do. You probably don't use a cream-separator, on a small farm like this. And I don't see any calves out there. It *must* be rich!" He smiled apologetically. "I can't drink coffee without it."

The elderly man turned his head away. "Mark! Milk for the coffee, please."

Slim dropped into a chair near the porch rail. "That hit the spot!"

"I'm glad to hear it." Phineas said mildly. Mark came with milk... came in the silence that had suddenly fallen over the gentle-mannered old man—over Satan—over the quiet, sleepy-eyed Slim. The servant set a small pitcher of rich milk on the table. Satan walked to the chair where Slim had carefully set his black cloak... a black cloak that was wrapped around a tommy-gun. The crew leader set his own garment over it.

"Take the gentlemen's things," Phineas ordered mildly. "Hang them inside, Mark."

"If you don't mind, we'll keep them right here," Satan said. His voice was quiet; but decided. Nevertheless, Mark started crossing to the chair. "I said, never mind," Satan told the man, his voice harder. The husky chap's face went taut; but Phineas called gently.

"That will do, Mark. You may go now."

Mark went. Satan came to the table, poured the creamy milk into his still steaming coffee. He added a lump of sugar from the bowl, stirred the Java gently.

"This *is* rich milk," he said evenly. "Why, the stuff looks almost *curdled!*"

Phineas nodded, his eyes serenely contemplating the peaceful scene in front of the bungalow.

Slim yawned, stretched sleepily, closed his eyes.

Satan didn't appear to notice. But he pulled his chair into a position where he could watch that front door. "I'll let my coffee sit until it's cooler," he said.

A SILENCE settled over the porch again. Satan was impelled to speak once; but he checked his question. Phineas stirred restlessly at a sound from inside the bungalow.

"You haven't taken your coffee yet—*Mr. Emory.*"

Satan wondered if the slight emphasis on his assumed name was his imagination. But he didn't let it show in his face. "I told you I was slow," he said, putting a chuckle into it. "I am inclined to take my time, so far as life is concerned, Mr. Phineas."

The older man's face was sober, his eyes unwinking. "I'm not," he said. But he smiled suddenly. "What a strange contrast! You—an apparently active, muscular, energetic man—are patient

111

and unhurried. While I, confined to an arm-chair or a wheel-chair, am impatient to go, to see, and to act!"

Satan coughed apologetically. "Excuse me, sir. Did you ever try to use—ah—artificial limbs? You might get more exercise, that way."

"You active men are sometimes unthinking men, as well," his host said. "Believe me, my friend, that the work of propelling this chair with my arms and hands is more than sufficient exercise."

"I should think so, now that you call it to my attention." Satan's voice was innocent; but his eyes were watchful. "Twenty years of that sort of thing will harden a man's hands and arms and chest, broaden his shoulders."

"Ah! Now you see what I mean?"

"Oh, yes," Satan smiled. "But, as you say, we active men—" he paused abruptly. "Our car was some miles *east* of town. We had a good long walk to get here... which was enough exercise for me."

"No one picked you up? Nothing passed you, on the way?"

"Two airplanes passed *over* us, as we walked along the road," Satan smiled. "You heard them here, of course?"

"Now that you mention it, I did hear something resembling an airplane motor. Just as it was beginning to get light. I was still in bed at the time."

"Much flying go on around here?" Satan asked.

"Very little." The man's manner was short. "Where are your friends coming from? Near here? Where did you tell them to meet you?"

Slim

"At the local hotel." Satan bent forward, his eyes serious. "I'm sure you won't mention our being here, until it's time for use to leave?"

"On my word, I shall not." The man laughed. "But, then—how could I?"

"Someone might call you and *ask*—on the telephone. Or your man Mark might mention it."

The man frowned. "We have no telephone here. I don't go in for that sort of civilized nuisance. But why do you ask that?"

"We're Government men," Satan confided. "Our visit here is official business."

Phineas laughed in a low, chuckling voice. "This is really more excitement than I am accustomed to!" he said, his eyes bright. "But won't you come inside and tell me something about your visit?"

Satan stood up, frowned at Slim. The man was in a deep sleep. "I think I'd better wake my friend."

"Let him sleep, let him sleep," Phineas said softly. "He is tired from his walk."

"All right," Satan agreed readily. "May I help you? Or would you prefer that Mark pushed your chair?"

"I can manage it myself," Phineas said quietly. "Mark is—busy."

A slight smile was on Satan's face, and his eyes were obviously admiring. "You're a wonder!" he said softly. "I don't see how you can manage to get your chair up that high step leading into the house!"

Phineas' face was suddenly averted. "I—I'm *so* absent-mind-ed," he murmured. "Silly of me, wasn't it?"

"I find it an expensive habit, myself—absent-mindedness," Satan said softly.

He pushed the wheel-chair to the door, leaned down and lifted it up the steep step as if it had been a matchstick. The door was only half open. Satan started the chair forward across the thick rug; but he stopped pushing suddenly, letting the thing coast.

As it cleared the door, Mark stepped swiftly from behind it. He blinked his surprise at something, then put out his hands to grip the handle. He continued pushing the thing to the large desk that stood over against one of the walls.

"Thank you, Mark," Satan said mildly.

THE CREW leader said admiringly, "This is a beautiful room, Mr. Phineas." He took in the rich rug, the costly furnishings of the place, the priceless vases that stood over the beautiful marble mantlepiece. "I would never have guessed, from the exterior of this bungalow, that such a gorgeous living room was concealed here."

But there was a coldness about the place, for all its richness, that brought a shiver to Satan—a coldness, and a darkness. He saw that there were rear windows; but that they were almost flat against the sharply rising hill, cutting off any light from that direction.

Mark pushed the chair behind the desk, which faced the room. But he had to remove the high-backed chair that was standing there, first. Satan looked at the rug closely, as if admiring its deep piling and the intricate colorings with which a dragon-like reptile was depicted on it... a design which was repeated on twin wall-hangings that flanked the desk. He scarcely noticed as the man Mark drifted away. He dropped into a chair near the desk.

"You're interested in what has us here, Mr. Phineas?"

"Decidedly." Satan didn't appear to notice the ice that had

come into the man's voice, didn't look around when he heard Mark walk quietly to the door letting onto the porch, come back stealthily into the middle of the room behind him.

Phineas' eyes didn't leave Satan's. But the crew leader was aware that man was waiting for something. Finally, he spoke.

"I'm decidedly interested—*Mr. Emory!* But first—would you mind putting your hands, palms down, on my desk?"

Satan appeared bewildered; but he did as he was asked.

"Thank you," Phineas said crisply. He smiled thinly, leaned forward as if taking Satan into his confidence. "You see, Mr. Government Agent—if you *hadn't* done as I requested, quietly and quickly—then Mark, who is behind you with his gun drawn, would have had to shoot you!" But his visitor didn't react properly.

"My, my!" Satan grinned good-naturedly. "And that would have spoiled your pretty rug, wouldn't it? The rug with the dragon design. Or—" his voice dropped to a whisper, "is it a *'newt'*—like your nickname... *Newt!* Is it a 'newt'... otherwise known as a *salamander!*"

Phineas' face drained of its good nature and its color. "You—you *devil,*" he gasped. "I thought you seemed too credulous, too uninquisitive! You're too dangerous to take any chances with! Mark—!"

There was the sudden, heavy crashing sound of a shot in the tense, cold room. A single, smashing sound, and acrid smoke crept into the air. A long-drawn sigh hung in the atmosphere for a moment, then the heavy thud of a falling body broke it short.

116

"Thank you, Slim," Satan said quietly, but his face going granite-hard. "That was a beautiful bit of timing!"

The man who called himself Phineas croaked, "You! *You!* But—but the coffee! You drank the coffee!"

Slim sauntered up, both capes on his arm and an automatic in his hand. "I didn't *drink* it," he said. "But that damned stuff nearly burned my skin off when I poured it down inside my collar."

Phineas was in a daze, shaking his head and muttering to himself. His eyes were wild as they went from one to the other of the men. Satan saw, arose, bowed low.

"I am afraid, Slim," he said in a gently chiding manner, "that we have disturbed Mr. Phineas by all this shooting." He turned to the legless man.

"We beg your pardon—*Emperor of the Dead!*"

## CHAPTER 14
## BOOMERANG SHOT

THE LITTLE, gray man seemed to shrink inches. His eyes fought with the terror that was in him, darted about the room as if in search of an escape. Satan was watching him closely.

"You might have had a better chance to put something over, Emperor," he said slowly, "if you had only kept your artificial legs on!"

The cripple glared balefully; but he tried to face Satan down. "You're crazy!" he said, trying to force his voice to be steady.

117

"I—I have no artificial legs! I—I just didn't think you were G-men. I thought you were two mobsters cracking down on me."

Satan's eyes were grim. "You've certainly picked up a lot of slang, sitting around in a wheel-chair, haven't you?" His eyes were contemptuous when he stared at the man. "But you made a big mistake when you pretended to be a wheel-chair invalid—but a self-sufficient one—one who didn't need much help."

The gray little man licked his lips, his eyes stricken. "What do you mean?" he whispered. "What mistake do you speak of?"

"Remember when I shook hands with you?" Satan asked. "A man who was in the habit of pushing the wheels of his chair would have had hard, calloused palms and fingers! A man who was in the habit of propelling a hard-tire chair across a thick-piled rug would have left marks on that rug—would have left tracks where the chair had rolled across the rug repeatedly."

The man blinked; but he didn't speak. Satan shook his head deploringly.

"Another thing was that chair behind the desk, which Mark had to clear out of of the way. I saw the marks the feet of it had dug into the rug, knew that you weren't in the habit of moving that chair to replace it with your wheel-chair."

Satan paused for a moment, then he said:

*"Another thing:* There are marks of *two* pairs of feet in this rug! A small pair… and those of your big-footed friend and gunner—Mark. *Another thing:* I wondered about you when I felt those soft hands; but my mind was made up when I saw that fresh milk *curdle* in the coffee. I realized that my guess was

right, that it *was* poisoned or doped coffee. But I didn't guess what big game I had until the name *'Newt'* struck me so forcibly… *newt* being another term for the salamander family." He paused, his face savage. "Is that enough—*Emperor?* Or do you want some more?"

The man sat crouched behind his desk, his hands dropping to the stumpy knees. Satan nicked his automatic out and jammed it close to him. "Up with those hands, you—or I'll blow your head into the wallpaper design!"

Phineas' face was ugly. But his hands went up slowly, stayed up. "Slim," Satan snapped. "Take a look at Mark, there—be sure he's cold! If you're satisfied that he is, have a look in the other rooms before we get down to business with Newt the First, or whatever the emperor styles himself."

Slim yanked the fallen gunner over, took one look at him. "Deader than a pickled herring," he said. Then he walked into the first of the two rooms opposite the desk.

He came out of that room, threw a pair of yellowish, artificial legs down on the rug next to Satan. "Here's the evidence," he said. He searched the other room, came back empty handed. "Just clothes and an assorted lot of junk."

Satan motioned him towards Phineas. "Lift him clear of his chair, Slim. Sit him on the desk. Then have a look under the cushion of that wheel-chair."

Slim did as he was told and came up with two gats. He pocketed the things, patted Phineas' clothes expertly, dug his hand inside the man's jacket and pulled another gun from an armpit holster. "Regular little arsenal," he observed mildly.

119

Captain Satan

"Strip him!" Satan said. "Right down to the skin. I'm not taking any chances with this warp-brained devil."

Phineas glowered as Slim ripped his coat, shirt and underwear loose. Satan smothered an exclamation and stepped nearer to peer at the man's skin. "What is that? A stain?" The man's body was colored a yellow-white.

Phineas didn't speak. Satan's eyes went hard as he waited, but still there was no answer. The crew leader clamped his mouth into a hard line and grasped his cigarette lighter in his hand. He snapped the flame alive and jammed it against the man's skin.

Phineas screamed his pain and tried to get away, setting his hands on the table and vaulting to the floor. He landed on his hands and the stumps of his knees and scuttled under the desk like a human crab. Satan shuddered his disgust. He reached under gingerly and pulled the monstrosity out. He plumped the man into a chair and stared at him.

"So! *You're* not a fire-cultist, anyway. Or, if you are—" He stopped, stared at the artificial legs, walked over slowly and picked them up. He turned them over, examined the soles of the feet carefully... sniffed at them. "What a hoax! Fire-proofed material, eh? This is how you do it!"

A smile of satisfaction was on his face when he turned to the man. "Where's the stain you use for your face? Come on, speak! You must have a removable stain to blend your face yellow-white with your legs and body." Still the man didn't speak, and Satan came near with his lighter.

"Don't," Phineas cried in terror. "Don't! I'll tell you, Mr. Desher!"

Slim and Satan stared at one another, then broke into a laugh.

The legless man glowered darkly, but he pointed to a drawer of his desk. "I keep it there," he said in a choked voice.

Satan pulled the drawer open. Inside it were several bottles of the stuff—and two hats with badges—badges that carried the legend—*"Gas Inspector."*

Satan tossed them onto the table, said, "Slim!"

The gaunt man looked, came close. "Well, I'm damned! The end of the trail, sure enough!"

The leader turned to the legless man. "That's our final bit of evidence," he said. "We know about those houses your gas inspectors set afire. And the money you have extorted from others. Are you going to talk? Or—?" He made a significant movement with the lighter.

"I'll—talk," the deformed man whispered brokenly.

SATAN POSTED Slim near the door, where he could watch for any signs of approach by Phineas' operatives… or the plane with the rest of Satan's crew.

"I—I lost my legs twenty years ago," the legless man told them, squatting bolt upright on his stumps in the big chair. "In the northern part of Japan. I was engaged in smuggling drugs to the States, during the war; and I lost my legs when I refused to pay a bandit a huge sum he demanded of me. I was left for dead. But I recovered, was getting around with artificial legs after three years."

Satan nodded. "That's where you collected your gang of fire-cultists?"

The man grew stubborn; but the threat of Satan's lighter loosened his tongue again. "Yes," he hissed. "That is true." His eyes grew reminiscent. "I was making my way through what I thought was a deserted old temple, looking for a confederate, when I came upon a group of fire worshipers in the midst of a ritual. I tried to escape when they rushed me. It is forbidden to look upon one of their ceremonies. But—" he shrugged his stumpy torso—"my legs defeated me… at first. And it came to me—the idea that saved my life!"

The man's eyes glittered as he recalled the scene. He licked his lips with satisfaction. "I told them, in their dialect, that I was a *yellow* fire god, and thus superior to their own. I talked to them, sang, chanted, as I stripped my clothes off. It was worth the try, anyway. *I walked through the fire, chanting.* And they believed… fell on their knees, adoring me!"

"And you turned them to your own uses? Used them for—extortion?"

The man shook his head. His face was composed, grave; but his eyes were watchful and furtive. "I saw I was burning my wooden legs, soon; for those cultists told others, and I had to repeat the act many times. Then one night, I made up my mind that I had to escape—had to get away. I knew their fanatical devotion to their religion, to their gods—*to me!* There was only one way I could escape. *I ordered them into the fire—to burn to death! And they obeyed me!*"

"Good God!" Satan breathed. He stared at the deformed man with wonder in his eyes. "But how is it they are with you—*were* with you, I mean—again?"

Phineas' eyes narrowed and a light of cunning came into them. But he continued smoothly: "I didn't go back to Japan again until last year. When I escaped the fire cultists, I came here—to Colorado—and roamed around seeking my fortune by my wits. I fell in with a man who told me of a natural gas well he had struck—but he thought the gas was worthless—*because the gas wouldn't burn!*"

"*Helium!*" Satan exclaimed.

"Helium," Phineas said in a low voice. "You are right! I then convinced the discoverer of the wells—Mark—that he should see the wisdom of my plan."

"What plan?" Satan inquired.

"The United States has an embargo on its sale of helium to foreign powers," the man said. "I wanted money—millions of dollars—and I could not have it through limited sale of the helium. I approached three great powers—but only one of them would talk *my* kind of money. And they would not advance to me the capital to refine the gas—to capture helium from the other gases with which it was mixed."

"Too much money," Satan hazarded. "That equipment costs plenty."

"Not that," the man shook his head. "That was not their objection. They were afraid the *transportation* of the gas would be detected. They feared that, if I was caught, the United States would find my wells—wells that have *ten percent* of helium gas in the raw state. They did not want the United States to be aware of the fact that such vast resources were here—right in the back yard, so to speak."

Satan's eyes were wide. "So you entered the extortion racket to get the money for the equipment? You planned to deliver it yourself."

The man nodded. "By operating a giant Zeppelin. I would fill a zeppelin with helium, fly the zep to my destination—the country with whom I would deal. There I would empty the dirigible of the helium—empty it into *tanks!* Then I would fill the zep—with hydrogen—and return to the well. There I would empty the craft of hydrogen—fill again with *helium*—and make another delivery!"

Satan shook his head in admiration. "What a plan! What an adventure! And you came so close to doing it!"

Phineas averted his eyes, wriggled around on the high-backed chair.

"Yes," he whispered. "It was so close... but for you! You—and that other one who calls himself—"

The man broke off, his face going toward the front windows. From outside came the drone of an airplane motor, clear but still far away. Slim turned and came into the room.

"The boys are coming," he said.

SATAN NODDED his satisfaction. "We'll go fast from here on," he said. "When the boys land, we'll want to be able to clear this place in a rush. I haven't forgotten that the—" he paused, his face turning to his lieutenant cagily—"the other boys from Washington are around, yet."

Slim nodded. "The Feds," he understood the crew leader to mean. The legless Emperor still thought that Satan was *Desher!*

The leader went to the capes which Slim had dumped into a chair. He felt around, came out with the cream-colored hydrogen bombs. "I think you overworked it when you used the rockets," he said. "But this is a neat trick."

Phineas stared, his eyes narrowed. "You know that, too? About the comets?"

Satan nodded. "You made a sucker play that time. Why?"

"Because my stupid subjects demanded a fitting bit of tribute to the departed—the *cleansed*—souls." He shrugged. "It was silly—but they insisted on something spectacular, a sky-high notice to their gods in the sun that more cleansed souls were on the way. And equally as stupid, I gave in."

Satan nodded his understanding. "But how about the houses you set afire? How did you work it?"

"My 'gas inspector'—the late departed Mark," he nodded to the corpse, "would gain admittance to the house, plant a hydrogen bomb, as you so aptly call it, and then he would hook up another metal container of hydrogen to the gas ranges in the kitchen."

"You rotten little monster!" Satan blazed, his eyes hard. "So when the cook had to turn on the stove for dinner—!"

The plane in the sky outside roared closer. Slim detected something peculiar about the sound of the motor, stepped to the door. "*Two* planes!" he shouted, excitedly. "Ours—and another, about five miles behind it!"

Satan's face was all business when he faced the deformed man again. "Get those legs on," he said. "I think I'll take you along with me—for certain purposes—until I get my hands on that money you've hijacked."

The man's face was hideous with rage. "I have none!"

126

Satan prodded the lighter at him. "Put your legs on," he said. "Get going!" He watched the man attach the things to the stumps, saw him draw a thin, skinlike material down from the stumps to cover the joints of the knee.

Slim picked up the two capes and the tommy-guns and moved them to a position nearer the door. He set the hydrogen bomb on a nearby table.

Phineas had dropped down into the high-backed chair again. The wheel-chair from which Slim had taken the two guns was ten feet from him. "All right," the man said, in a resigned voice. "—"

He put his hands on the seat of the chair and pushed himself up—but in his hand an automatic appeared.

Satan fired from the hip; but it was too late. The little man had pulled the trigger of his gun and put a shot squarely into the hydrogen bomb—a split second before his hand was smashed by Satan's slug.

His scream blended with the crash of the gas container, and a sheet of smoke and flame raced across the room, devouring everything in its path. Slim grabbed for his tommy-gun, but the flames swirled around him. He snatched up the Satan-lamp from the floor near the chair and backed farther into the room as the blaze crept closer to him.

Satan was raising his gun to blast the deformed monster when Phineas screamed, "Don't shoot! Don't shoot! There is an escape!"

The man swayed across to one of the wall hangings, jerked

it out of the way, revealed a metal door in the wall. He pressed a button and the portal swung open. "This way!" he snapped.

Satan looked around him, and Slim ranged up at his side. The room was a raging inferno with but a small space left for them... and that would be gone in a split second. He swung his eyes to the back windows... the windows that were almost flat against the hill that ranged up inches from the bungalow. He suddenly saw that they were dummies—false windows painted on the wall!

No escape there! He was aware of a sudden cold draught on his back... swung to see Phineas standing in a tunnel cut in solid rock; and trying to swing a rear door shut.

The crew leader jumped for it, managed to wrest it open again; but he lost his gun doing it. Slim, close on his heels, turned for a moment. He poised himself carefully... swung the Satan lamp on a hard line through the flames, like a skilled horseshoe thrower pitching for the stake. But he was aiming for the door.

"I hope it goes out through the door!" he muttered. "The gang *may* find it. It will tell them we're in the vicinity."

Then, suddenly, an unseen hand whipped that door shut with a crash, knocking the lieutenant flat on his back.

They looked about them, then, and saw that they were in a seemingly long passage. They couldn't see the other end of the tunnel, for everything was as black as pitch.

A crazed laugh rang out farther down the passage. Satan, his eyes squinting, followed a bend, stopped in his tracks. There was a lighted chamber ahead, a chamber in which Phineas stood, his face peering into the darkness of the passage, a crafty grin on his features.

And ranged behind him were a dozen or more naked forms that walked in a slow, chanting file through a mat of living flame. Satan gasped.

"My God! What is this?" But he knew the answer to his own question. He knew now, too late, that he was facing a ritualistic ceremony of Phineas' fire-cultists!... Trapped between two fires, under the Colorado hillside... unarmed... with madmen waiting for them at the end of the lane.

## CHAPTER 15
## LAST CHANCE

**B**ACK AT the hideout near Thatcher, Kayo had bundled the crew into the plane after starting Solly away in the car, with the G-man safely stowed into the back seat and tied securely out of sight.

"Jump over to a deserted ranch, someplace," the husky driver told the hawk-nosed member of the crew. "Dig up a good hideout and keep this G-man holed in. But don't make it farther than a radius of twenty miles from here. When and if we come back this way, we'll circle a wide area and you come out and signal us. Be sure you signal the right plane!"

"Oi! You betcha, Kayo." The weazened man considered. "And what if you don't come back at all, ever?"

Kayo grinned. "Then you start earning your keep!" he said.

Solly got under way and Kayo slammed the cabin door and

gave the ship her full gun. He roared into the sky as the sun nosed up onto the horizon.

Soapy

Doc

Emperor
of Death

Kokamori

But the plane hadn't been twenty minutes under way when Pat, staring overside, growled: "Kayo! There's another o' these sky buggies loose! Look at 'er, coming up from the direction of Thatcher! It's an open job!"

The burly, swarthy driver and pilot for Satan stared down... saw the ominous puffs of smoke that jetted from the nose of that other ship. "G-men," he sang out. "Boys, we're in for it! That plane ain't any slouch, or I don't know my ailerons! We can't slip 'em, not in the short run we're makin'. An' I'm damned if I'm going to quit before I hit that field where we left Cap'n and Slim. Nothing less'n a miracle will bring me down short of there!"

Straight ahead, the crew plane roared, nose dipping as low as possible, to jam on all the speed that Kayo could muster. The big fellow looked back often, over the course of the next twenty miles, gauged the comparative speed of that other ship.

"He can't catch us, anyway," he grunted.

"Maybe they'll radio ahead, and some other plane will hop up to head us off," Gentleman Dan wondered. He sat back in a rear seat, his wounded leg perched up over The Dutchman's shoulder, where he sat directly in front of Dan.

"Listen, Dan," Kayo said, turning his masked face back. "This ain't no civilized country. It's all prairie, or sumpin'! The first good town we come to is where Slim an' Cap'n left off."

They drilled on steadily, Kayo nursing every mile of speed he could get out of the plane. Doc, looking ahead, stirred and said mildly:

"Is that the town, ahead there? To the right a bit?"

Kayo swung, started to nose down to come in low and save all the time he could. He didn't want to glide down for a long landing, nor did he feel like coming down in a steep dive. He cocked his eyes back at the pursuing ship, nosed down still further until he was running all out.

Gentlemen Dan had come erect, was staring straight ahead on their route. "Look, Kayo," he said. "I'm not much use on the ground, right now. Suppose, when you land, I jump the plane off and keep it in the air until you locate Cap'n and Slim, if they're not at the field where you dropped 'em?"

"Huh? Can you fly, too?"

Gentleman Dan laughed. "A couple of dozen Germans could answer that, if they were still alive," he said. "Don't worry about me—*or* the ship!"

Pat yelped, "Look, Kayo! There's a house on fire, below there! Do you think that can have anything to do with them?"

Kayo shook his head. "Naw." But he circled, made an easing turn without slacking speed. He looked over his shoulder at Gentleman Dan, a worried crease between his eyes. "What's your plan when we land, Danny?"

"You watch!" the debonaire member grinned. "I figure the Federals will want to land and see what we're up to in that town—so they won't follow the ship. I'll fix things. Don't worry!"

Kayo grinned, turned. They were coming low, nearing the town, were flashing across its border. Everybody in the cabin jumped when Doc rose in his chair and said. "My God! Look! That black barn! See it—on the side, there?"

Kayo skidded the bus expertly off line to snatch a look.

The next second, the pilot cursed fluently and stuck the plane into a steep slip. He ruddered in for a landing in the pasture, near that black barn on which the eyes of them all were fastened.

IN THE rear seat of the speedy, open-pit job, Jo Desher, Chief of the F.B.I., bit savagely into his unlighted cigar and howled for more speed. The pilot raised his hands in a helpless gesture and drilled on.

Desher had fired a few futile volleys at the plane that sped ahead of him; but he might have been a kid shooting spitballs at an express train for all the attention he got. After a while he quit.

But his face was ugly when he saw the front plane shoot down for a landing, near a flaming building below. "I knew it!" he roared. "I knew Satan was in this burning and extortion business someplace!" But he felt a distinct pang of regret that his old rival *could* be placed in such a dastardly role.

The cabin plane was going down sharply, now; but it was still miles ahead of Desher's plane. He shouted frantically to the pilot to get the crate down, then sat back in his pit to check his automatics and his cartridge clips.

Suddenly, the pilot pounded on the cockpit coaming. Desher looked up. The man was pointing. The F.B.I. agent stared, cursed suddenly, rubbed his goggles and stared again.

There, on the grass a short distance in front of that burning house was a black square of some sort, "Like a *camera*," Desher thought. But he yelled, "It's a Satan-lamp!" when he shifted his eyes to the side of that black barn.

There, in bold relief, was a circle of light—a circle of light out of which Satan was charging, with pitchfork raised. The beam was coming from the lamp on the ground!

"Set 'er down," Desher roared excitedly. "Set 'er down!"

The pilot fishtailed in for a speedy landing. The other ship was already on the ground, and men were pouring from its open cabin door. The G-man's pilot nosed down slightly, was settling for a landing.

And suddenly that other plane swung into action, whipped around in a fast turn on the ground, and raced straight for the plane the G-man's pilot was trying to set down!

Desher cursed when his pilot zoomed frightenedly. "To hell with him! Don't chase him! Get the plane down!"

INSIDE THE darkened tunnel, Satan snapped to Slim: "Strip! This is a desperate chance, but it's our last one. Strip and rub this yellow stain on your body, head, shoulders and face. I'm stripping, too—but I'm not using any stain. I have another plan!" He handed Slim the bottle of stain—the dye the Emperor used—which he still held in his hand.

In one hand, Satan gripped the barrel-shaped automatic cigarette lighter—the lighter that had *two* uses; for, on the bottom of it, there was a Satan-beam that worked on a tiny but strong battery. In the other hand was folded the mask, which he had taken from one of his pockets.

"I dropped my gun when I went to pick up the tommy," Slim said in a whisper.

Phineas was roaring down to them....

"Come, my brilliant detective! Come—and bring your friend—if he isn't roasting to death in the flames of the bungalow!" The man laughed crazily. "You'd take my money, would you? It doesn't matter if you have a gun! I'll send my subjects in after you! They'll rush you, and you won't be able to kill all of them! Come!"

"Forget the gun," Satan said tensely. "It wouldn't have helped, anyway. We'll handle this thing the only way we can. Boldly— unafraid!" He paused. "You got that stain on you yet?"

"Right, Captain."

Satan tensed, listening to the sing-song chant of Phineas as he addressed his subjects. "…Two foul, impure ones who have come to regain their gold," he said, his voice raging. "They come with guns. They do not know that the subjects of the Emperor of the Dead will brave the guns to seize and cleanse these impure ones!"

"We brave anything in the service of thee, sire," the men made sing-song answer in their Oriental language.

"Quick, Slim!" Satan snapped. "Walk in—go on! I'm follow- ing right behind you. This man has missed one bet, and I'm staking all on that!" As Slim started forward, Satan hissed, "And chant! Sing!"

"Sing, Captain? What'll I sing? You know I can't carry a tune!"

"Sing, Slim—or, by God, your flesh will be singing over an open fire before you're ten minutes older! Sing, Slim!"

Slim went grimly but shakily ahead, his eyes bulging large when he saw the mat of burning coals in that flare-lit chamber.

Satan came rapidly behind him, crouched, hiding from the men inside behind Slim's gaunt and naked figure.

And Slim chanted as he went, the growing cold of the place sending his teeth in a mad chatter. The gaunt man faltered when he came to the end of the passage, saw Phineas seated on a raised throne, saw the frowning Orientals who lined the wall under a row of flares. So *this* was the den of the Emperor of the Dead!

Bikko the Firemaker was squatted grotesquely at the bed of coals, fanning the flames higher.

Slim was in the room, Phineas signaled to two of the men by the wall. Satan listened to him speak in that Japanese dialect of the brown men, heard him say….

"Seize this skeleton of a one, first! He—" But the Emperor broke off, his eyes going wide as they fell on Slim's glistening, yellow-white skin… skin that was the same color as that of the Emperor of the Dead himself.

Satan saw his chance, called from his darkened hiding place in the narrow passage: "Stop, my children! Touch not the holy body of one of the greater Fire Gods! I, too, am sacred, and a lord over my subjects!"

The man on the throne gagged, then screamed: "He lies! He lies! Test him with the flames, O my subjects! Let him walk the flames unafraid and unharmed, if he does not lie!"

In the sudden confusion, Satan slipped from his hiding place and slid to a dark corner. He waited, tense, as Slim stood there.

The Emperor screamed again. "See? He lies! He lies! I tell you, he is afraid of flames—cannot walk on even the simple bed of coals! Test him! Try him!"

Several of the men stepped forward uncertainly. And then

Satan gambled all, pressed the switch of his lighter. He held the light in front of him and pointed the beam towards a wall at his back. The entire line of men gasped when a light sprang into being in that corner, a light that bloomed as suddenly as though the walls had melted away to admit it.

The Emperor of the Dead came to his feet, tottered down from the throne, holding his throat and gasping.

On the wall was that circle of greenish light with the black head of Satan in its center, pitchfork raised in a terrifying threat. And standing chalk white against that dread background was Satan himself, his starkly magnificent physique clear-etched in every rippling muscle of his great arms and chest and shoulders—his face hidden in the shadows.

"Move not!" Satan sang out in sonorous voice… and in the dialect of the brown men. "The Great One Himself has come, to take charge of you, his subjects!"

## CHAPTER 16
## DEATH HAS COLD FINGERS

SATAN AND Slim stood as if turned to stone. The effect on the brown men was immediately evident. Mouths wide, eyes staring, they trembled as they looked on what they thought was a miracle of their faith—the coming of The Great One!

One of the brown men uttered a strangled cry and prostrated himself on his face. Instantly, the whole line of them moved, stretched out in humble adoration in front of that dread figure.

But the Emperor of the Dead was fighting for his sanity…

Slim pointed at the
speeding blaze of light.

and for his life and fortune. "Satan!" he screamed. "So you *were* Satan, and not Desher!" His wild terror and rage blended in a series of ear-piercing shrieks. Then he started an incoherent babble in the brown men's dialect.

Satan snapped in English, "Shut up, you fool! Don't you know that at one word these men would tear you limb from limb? Are you ready to bargain, or do you want to take a nice sleep on that fire mat?"

The Emperor looked fearfully at his "subjects." They were still prostrated on the earth. "What—what do you want of me?" he croaked.

"What is this set-up here?" Satan asked severely. "Talk fast!" But in an aside, he said to the brown men: "Remain prostrate, dogs—until I speak the word. The one who first raises his head until I command it shall be cleansed!"

"Where did you learn all this?" the Emperor of Death whispered. "I—I thought I was the only one knew their secrets!"

"I suppose you thought you were the only man who had ever been in Japan and China, and who had seen the primitive fire cultists or knew of their strange faith?" Satan laughed unpleasantly. "Come on, Phineas. Speak up while you have the chance."

"This is the whole set-up," the man moaned. "This is where the helium wells were found, and where I'm refining the gas."

"What?" Satan saw that the men were unmoving. "You're refining the gas, here? Now?"

Slim said softly, "Maybe that's why this place is so darned cold, Captain, in spite of the fire!"

Satan snapped a look at the Emperor. "You have gas washing

140

and cleaning equipment here? Where?" The cowering man indicated a wall with a feeble hand. At a sign from his chief. Slim went to the spot, peered, found an iron handle cleverly concealed in the rock wall. He yanked on it.

A section of the wall came open. "It's hinged, like a door," Slim said. He pulled the thing wide.

Satan smothered a gasp of surprise. An entire gas refining plant was in that other chamber... a plant that could be handled by a crew of twelve men, just like the government plant that Satan had once seen at Amarillo, Texas. And it could operate at full capacity.

He was starting to question further when a hammering came at the iron door down the passage.

"K-O! K-O!" came the muffled shout of a code signal.

Satan started, snapped an order at one of the prostrated men. "The dog among you who opens the door... *rise!*"

Bikko the Firemaker came from his hunched crouch; but with his eyes averted from that dazzling figure in the light of that corner.

"Go! Open!" Satan spoke in the man's dialect.

He said to Slim, "You follow him, to make sure the boys don't jump the chap. And lock the door after you, when you're all inside."

"Right, Captain."

Slim, Bikko and the crew were in the great cavern in the space of a minute. The Emperor of the Dead watched in terror as man after man of Satan's Crew filed in. Satan checked each with his eyes as they came...

141

"…Pat… Kayo… Doc… The Dutchman… Soapy." He stopped. "Where are the others?"

Kayo told him, "Solly is with the G-man. Gentleman Dan took our plane off, when the Feds were landing. He scared them up again, and gave us time to get to this door."

"But how did you get here, with the house burning?"

"It's out," Kayo said. Slim nodded confirmation. "The whole thing is burned to ashes, Captain. We spotted the lamp. It was shining on the wall of the barn."

Satan considered. "How many Federals were there?"

"Only two—in that plane. I could swear the guy in the rear pit was Desher," Kayo said.

Another hammering came at the iron door. "The F.B.I.," a voice hailed faintly. "Open up, Satan! I've got a hundred men here!"

"He's nuts!" Kayo growled. "He's all alone. One man with him, at best."

Satan's eyes gleamed in the light of the mat of coals. He spoke to Bikko again, in his native tongue. "Admit the one who comes," he said. He told his men—"Back up into that recess over against that wall, out of sight."

To the rest of the brown men he said, "Line up with your backs flat to the wall so that he who comes in can be seized. But do him no harm!"

Bikko came running low, in a crouch, ahead of Desher. The F.B.I. chief pounded down the dark tunnel, his voice uttering threats ahead of him….

"The game's up, Satan!" he was roaring. "A hundred men are

at my back! Lay down your guns or, by God, we'll shoot the living daylights out of you!"

The man hove into view of the glowing mat of coals, paused, then stepped into the chamber. And the brown men swarmed down on him and bore him to the ground.

Satan slipped his mask on swiftly.

Desher's gun went off, without harming anybody, before it was twisted from his hand. Satan barked an order and the brown men climbed to their feet, still holding Desher fast.

Satan smiled, his masked face contemplating the G-man. "Desher, let me present you to a man whose acquaintance we have both sought—the man who caused comets to flare and houses to burn and who extorted money—who framed a three-cornered trap which brought you and Kokamori and me to grips! The man who caused the death of the Jap naval spy, and of a dozen of *your* men—and of one of my best." He bowed ironically in the direction of the cowering cripple.

"Desher—meet the *Emperor of the Dead!*"

IT WAS with doubting eyes that Desher listened to the tale of the helium unfold, and of the man who styled himself the Emperor—the Emperor of the Dead.

"A lot of Mullarkey. Why, these guys don't even *look* like Japs! Look at 'em."

"Primitive type," Satan said. "From the North Provinces. Want to see some proof, Desher?" He spoke to the men in the peculiar tongue. The F.B.I. man paled as one after another of the men walked slowly through the freshened flames. But Desher tried to be hard-boiled.

"Circus stuff!" he sneered. Then he looked around. "What makes this place so cold, with that fire going? That's just one of the angles of this that I can't understand!"

Satan grinned. "You ought to know how cold a helium plant can be! The Emperor of the Dead has a nice one; and it's going full blast, too. Have a look." He added, "It's cold, because it isn't well insulated."

The G-man's eyes were frankly disturbed when he came from the refining room. Satan stared at him, chuckled a bit. "Ready to listen?"

Desher nodded, his head bent and his eyes on the fire.

When Satan had concluded telling of the Emperor's plans, the F.B.I. man said, "I've got to admit it sounds logical enough. But how in hell you ever figured it out—" He broke off, made his voice brusque. "But, one way or another, you'll have to be taken into custody, along with the others."

Satan laughed heartily. But he turned suddenly to the Emperor. "Where's the money—the rest of the swag?"

"It's gone," the man said sullenly.

"You lie!"

"Well, *you'll* never find it!" the man snarled. But he fell silent at Satan's smile. The crew leader turned to Bikko.

"Where does the Emperor of the Dead—he who is my slave!—keep the gold he has taken from the impure ones?"

Bikke salaamed low, and answered, "In the wall, O Great One—in the wall inside the great fire that cleanses." He pointed to the glowing door at the far end of the room. Satan commanded Bikko to go and open it. But he started at the roaring flames that came from that space.

"Ah!" he said after a moment. "So that's it!" He turned to Desher. "Phineas—the Emperor, to you—has to use up the fuel gas that's left, after he isolates the helium from the other gasses. He can't sell it—or people would know of the wells under this hill." He shrugged. "So he burns it… burns *people* in it, too, I imagine. And he keeps his money safe in a wall protected by the flames."

The Emperor screamed curses at Satan, howled to his men that their "Great One" was a fraud. The brown men were frowning, staring at Satan, at Desher, at the other "infidels" who crowded the room.

Satan shook his head, said to the Emperor of Death, "You fool! I tried to save you from it. But it's you or me, now—and I guess you know what the answer is!"

"No, no!" the man moaned, grovelling on the earth. "The money is in a strongly protected wall safe. The wall safe in that fire chamber! All you need do to open it is shut off the fuel-gas outlet in the refinery—a ten-inch pipe, with blue bands around it!"

"You're too late," Satan told him grimly. "Climb up on that fire bed and walk through it!"

The man got to his feet, trembling. Satan said, in the dialect: "The dog refuses to walk the fires of purification!"

"I'll walk!" the Emperor of the Dead sobbed.

He climbed onto the bed of fire, made his way rapidly through

The brown men struggled
with the head of the G-Men.

it. Now the brown men were plainly suspicious, and came

threateningly nearer to Satan. The crew leader shouted at them.

"Back, dogs! Back! You doubt my word? Seize him, whom you call Emperor of the Dead! Seize him, I say. Tear off his legs—which are not legs—and then cause him to walk the fires!" He signaled his men, who were standing with their tommy-guns at ready, to wait.

Bikko the Firemaker stared at Satan, then twisted his over-large head to look at the Emperor of the Dead, to stare at his legs. "It is not permitted to touch the person of the Emperor," he said to Satan.

"Tear off his legs that are not legs, I say!" Satan thundered.

Bikko loped over in his grotesque crouch, set a hand on one of the man's legs, and jerked suddenly. The Emperor toppled sideways as his artificial right leg was wrenched off at the knee. The rest of the brown men exclaimed in surprise, then with a shout of savage hatred at the fallen man, sprang up.

Satan said tensely, "It's tough to watch a thing like this. But it's either his life or the slaughter of these poor devils if they attack us."

"Maybe they won't attack," Desher suggested hopefully.

"There's no question about it," Satan told him quietly. "I know these people, and their rituals. They're a secret, primitive people who practice the religion of Japanese savages of a thousand years ago. If we don't let them kill the Emperor, they'll attack us. Besides—the Emperor wasn't squeamish about all those people he burned to death."

Bikko came near Satan, salaamed low. "We wish to cleanse the foul dog," he said.

148

"Cleanse him," Satan ruled, in a low voice.

The Emperor of the Dead screamed horribly as Bikko's strangling hands went out for him. The entire group, Satan and his crew and Desher, watched as the struggling man was borne to the glowing door... saw the portal

wrenched back... heard the quavering scream with which The Emperor of the Dead plunged out of sight.

The door clanged shut again.

Satan broke the silence. "Shut the valve of the ten-inch pipe, Slim."

Desher growled, "I thought you didn't take money that belonged to honest people!"

"Honest people?" Satan smiled. "If the people who were being shaken down hadn't come across, if they had gone to the police,

Phineas wouldn't have been able to get away with this. They supported this fiend. I have no sympathy for them."

He laughed. "What are you kicking about? You're going to be able to make Uncle Sam a present of the richest helium well in the whole world!" He coughed slightly. "In two days."

Desher asked, "Where are you taking me until then?"

"No place," Satan told him calmly. "I'm leaving you to the watchful care of my subjects."

Desher's eyes went round. "Hey, now! Listen, Satan—you can't do this to me! These devils will roast me alive!"

Satan's stare was frigid. "Will you promise to shut your mouth for two days? Will you give me a chance to get away with the loot? Will you give my man, who was killed at Thatcher, a decent burial?"

"I'll give that big fellow a decent burial," Desher said. "I was going to, anyway."

"But you won't let me get away?"

"Hell, no! I'll go after you the minute I get free—whether that's tomorrow—this minute—or when I meet you in Hell."

Satan grinned. "Stout feller, Desher! My hat's off to you."

"I'd rather it was your mask."

Satan told the brown men to secure Desher's watch; but the F.B.I. man passed it quickly when they started into his pockets. Then the leader spoke to them long and carefully.

"I told them," Satan said, "to keep you here in good health and with food until the short hand of the watch has made four circles. In other words, forty-eight hours. There's only one specification: the pilot you have outside is going to keep you company."

Desher nodded. "I can't help myself," he said miserably.

"Yes, you can! Just don't argue with the men, or try to shoot them. I'm leaving you your gun—in case something slips. But it's on your oath not to use it except in self-defense. These chaps aren't criminals, Desher. They're poor, deluded, cusses who are trying to do their best. Promise?"

"I promise," Desher said.

"Shut off the gas, get the dough, bring in the pilot," Satan said to his men. They immediately started to work.

## CHAPTER 17
## TRAIL'S END

THE BUZZER of Cary Adair's sky-high penthouse apartment rang insistently. Cary sighed, put down his volume of "Arabian Nights," in the original Iranic, and got to his feet.

Adair smiled slightly, crossed the soft rug and went through the portières. He opened the door himself. He smiled at the man in the entrance.

"Hullo, Jo!" he said. "Come in!"

Desher burst into the room. "Where've you been for the last few days?"

"Where have *I* been? Why, right here!"

"Like hell! A call was made to my New York Bureau. It was

traced to this number. My men called here, but there was no answer!"

Adair shrugged. "Oh, that! Yes; Jeremy called. To let you know that the poor chap, the hallman—who had been in that—er—*mess* you caused up here—*had died!*"

"Good God!" The F.B.I. man blinked. "Did the burns do it?"

"Burns did it," Adair said. "But strangely, his *house* was burned to the ground shortly after he went home. I buried him, of course—and gave his widow a suitable pension. Felt I had to, y'know. Sort of up to me, since *you* caused him all that grief."

Desher growled, "Listen, I just got through paying a thousand bucks to bury a guy I never laid eyes on before. What are *you* bellyaching about?"

"Mainly about Jeremy," Adair yawned. "The man came down with an attack of something that looks like a cross between the heaves and yellow jaundice. He's been in bed for—"

"I beg pardon, sir. I'm up, sir; and at your service." The tall man stood in the doorway. His face and the skin of his hands were a strange-yellow-white color.

"Ah, Jeremy!" Adair beamed, rubbed his hands together, dropped into his chair. "Now I can relax again."

A few minutes later, after Jeremy had served drinks, Adair grinned.

"How are your Japanese friends, Jo?"

"Oh, they're okay," Desher growled.

"And—the Emperor of the Dead, as you so quaintly termed him?"

Desher glowered. "Say! If you'd been—" He stopped.

"Well?"

"If you'd been as busy as I have the last few days, you wouldn't be talking fairy tales—or dreams!"

"Oh! The Emperor was just a dream?"

Desher downed his drink and jumped to his feet. "Seems like that to me, now." He let Jeremy help him into his coat; but he shuddered when he looked at the strange pallor of the man's face. When Jeremy had gone, Adair said:

"What's wrong between you and Jeremy? You looked positively sickened, when you thanked him for helping you."

Desher shuddered. "I've come to hate yellow—*or brown!*"

The immaculate Adair grinned. "A few doses of salts should—er—*cleanse* him thoroughly!"

"Don't use that word," Desher moaned.

"What word?"

"Cleanse!"

Adair grinned as he turned his head to look after Jeremy. "You know something, Jo? To-morrow is Jeremy's birthday. He admires your watch no end. Just because it's yours, I suspect. Give it to him, like a good fellow, and I'll replace it with one twice the value."

Desher shook his head. "I—I can't do it," he said. "You see—I gave my watch to some—ah—friends who were going to Japan."

"Well," Adair sighed. "Don't bother."

"Listen, Cary—this Jap—er—I mean friend, did plenty for me. Besides, he was a strange little hunchbacked fellow and he took such a shine to the ticker that I decided to let him have it."

153

"Wise decision," Adair murmured, following Desher to the door. "Toodle-oo, old man. Stop up again when you can. But don't bring any more fires with you."

"You're telling me!"

**ADAIR COCKED** an eye at Jeremy. "You heard? You managed it?" And the man answered, "Very simply, sir. A thousand dollars... in small bills. I put it in the inside pocket of his jacket, sir." Jeremy dusted an invisible speck from Adair's lapel.

"Coffee, sir?" he murmured. "With a little—ah—*milk?*"

Adair grinned and walked to the studio window, stared out over the bay. "I hope you get your—er—*color* back soon, Jeremy!" Then he said, "Don't develop this last photo of Desher. I can do without him for a time!"

*"Very—GOOD, sir,"* Jeremy barked happily.

www.ingramcontent.com/pod-product-compliance
Lightning Source LLC
Chambersburg PA
CBHW052139170626
46812CB00004B/1509